RESCUED BY THE ALIEN WARRIOR

HOPE HART

The Arcav Alien Invasion Series

The Arcav King's Mate

The Arcav Commander's Human

The Arcav General's Woman

The Arcav Prince's Captive

A Very Arcav Christmas

The Arcav Captain's Queen

The Arcav Guard's Female

The Warriors of Agron Series

Taken by the Alien Warrior

Claimed by the Alien Warrior

Saved by the Alien Warrior

Seduced by the Alien Warrior

Protected by the Alien Warrior

Captured by the Alien Warrior

Rescued by the Alien Warrior

Enticed by the Alien Warrior

Conquered by the Alien Warrior

CHAPTER ONE

Zoey

I'm stumbling, walking as if in a fog. I feel as if I'm floating above my body and no longer in control of it.

My arms and legs are working, but it's like I'm a puppet, the movements jerky and uncoordinated.

How did this happen to me?

I'm a good person. I swear. I'm not a saint, but I donate to charity. I check on my neighbors. I never cheat or steal.

How did I end up here?

My face feels wet, and I reach up, finding tears streaming from my eyes. I'm sobbing, and I can no longer see where I'm going.

I trip, and one of the other women reaches out to steady me, but it's too late. I fall to my knees.

I attempt to get to my feet, but something hits me in the ribs so hard I can hear the crack.

Pain swims through me, and bile creeps up my throat. One of the other aliens drags me to my feet, almost impaling me with his horns as he snaps at his friend.

Then I'm hunched over, barely able to breathe through the pain as we walk toward the ship that will take us to our fate.

Time jumps.

I choke, gasping. My chest is aching, my body shaking with chills.

My fractured ribs no longer allow me to breathe deeply, and my lungs are filling with fluid.

I'm drowning, suffocating here in this godforsaken cage on this godforsaken planet.

Alone.

I jolt awake, my lungs burning as I choke. I'm damp with sweat, and I sit up, gasping for air.

My kradi is silent as I tremble and pant.

This is one of the main reasons I insisted on moving out of the healers' kradi. Not only was I sick of being treated like a patient, but there's nothing worse than coming awake screaming or choking for air only to find sympathetic eyes appraising you like you're a wounded dog in the pound.

I shudder.

It takes me another long moment before I can get to my feet and peek outside. The sun is rising, and there's no way I'll be able to get back to sleep. I pull off the gauzy shift I sleep in and wipe myself down with a damp cloth. Once I'm no longer sweating, I pull on a simple gray dress and grab my basket.

Within a few minutes, I'm in the forest.

My hands don't shake here. My body isn't tense. Technically, I'm supposed to take a guard with me for these little trips, but I need this. I need the solitude, the sounds of the wind rustling through leaves, the feel of the dead branches crunching beneath my feet.

Distantly, I can hear an animal rooting around in the underbrush, and the earthy scent of decomposing leaves helps me shake off the nightmares.

The memories.

I don't dare wander too far. I may need this time to myself, but I'm not an idiot. Sure, we managed to fight off the Dokhalls when they came back for us. But none of us truly believes it's over. We saw them scatter when they realized they'd lost the battle, but I bet they're busy figuring out their next plan.

My shoulders slump. When *will* it be over?

It's not enough that they stole us from our planet. That one of them kicked me hard enough to crack my ribs, leading to pneumonia that nearly killed me. No, they had to come back, tracing the ship we crash-landed in so they could load us onto their new ship, along with the group of human women they were transporting to whatever fresh hell awaited them.

A branch cracks, and I whirl, my eyes meeting cool blue-green.

"Sarissa." My hand flies to my chest.

"Sorry, I didn't mean to disturb you. I thought I'd sneak out for a walk. Obviously we're on the same page."

I smile. Sarissa is Vivian's cousin, and the two women spent hours both laughing and crying when they reunited. They're attempting to figure out how they were both taken. I mean, what are the chances?

I think all of us are trying to understand it. Why us? Why *do* bad things happen to good people?

I examine her. She looks just like Vivian—gorgeous. But while Vivian never has a hair out of place, Sarissa has an earthy, natural beauty. Her hair is in a simple ponytail, and she gives the impression she'd laugh at you if you asked her to put on makeup.

She examines me through ocean eyes. "What are you collecting?"

I point at the small bush. "Ortar. The leaves are a natural antiseptic when they're crushed and turned into a paste."

"Wow."

Sarissa reaches out and helps me pick a few of the leaves. "How'd you learn about this?"

"I was sick. I've spent most of my time on Agron in the healers' kradi, and I'm a nurse on Earth. So I was naturally curious, I guess."

"Is this an invite-only party, or can anyone join?"

We both turn as Vivian strolls through the trees. She's wearing a deep-purple dress that makes her look like a queen.

I sigh. "Well, there goes my peaceful, quiet morning."

She smirks at me. "You want peace and quiet? Don't expect to find it in a barbaric camp on Agron."

I nod at the sheathed dagger she has tied to the pretty blue belt around her waist. "Where'd you get that?"

"Lifted it from the weapons kradi."

My eyes widen, and Sarissa laughs, throwing her arm around Vivian.

"A few months on this planet and my cousin is turning into a savage. Who would've thought?"

Vivian rolls her eyes but grins at me, and I can't help but grin back. When we first met, I was intimidated by the woman with the sharp tongue who seemed so put together. But since we've been here, Vivian has mellowed in a lot of ways.

And obviously, she has hardened in others.

I pick a few more leaves and add them to my basket. We wander through the forest until we get to a tall tree with bright white flowers hanging above our heads.

Sarissa glances at me. "Poisonous?"

I smile at that. On this planet, we tend to assume everything is poisonous.

"I have no idea. I've never seen them before."

The flowers are dangling from a thin branch, but they're too high for us to reach, and I pout. Maybe I can come back and climb the tree another time.

Vivian glances at my face and sighs. "Stand back," she says, pulling her knife _from_ her belt. She narrows her eyes at the tree, then throws the knife, the movement almost casual. My mouth drops open as the knife hits the thin branch with pinpoint accuracy, and a few of the flowers fall to the ground.

I stare at her. "What was that?"

She shrugs, and Sarissa laughs while I use a rag to pick up the flowers, careful not to touch them with my bare skin.

"I'll take them back to the healers' kradi and ask Moni about them." I tilt my head. "That knife is stuck in the tree. You'll need a new one." It's too high for us to reach, the blade buried in the bark.

Sarissa smiles. "Don't worry. She'll get a new one."

There's more to Vivian than I'd ever thought, but she hunches her shoulders as I stare at her, so I change the subject. "How are you feeling?"

Vivian rolls her eyes, and I can't help but laugh at her

mock sigh of annoyance. "I swear, if anyone else asks me that..."

"No pain, then?"

"No. I owe those bastards payback for my new scar though."

Vivian saved Nevada's life during the battle and nearly died herself. I shudder as I remember the bone-chilling fear that hit me when I saw just who was being carried into the healers' kradi that day.

"Zoey."

We all turn at the deep rumble. Sarissa raises one eyebrow at me. "Caught," she mutters.

Tagiz stands next to a large white tree, disapproval written all over his face. Even with his brow furrowed in a deep scowl, he's still the most attractive man I've ever seen.

His eyes are gray and piercing, and the ridge of his brow bone would make him look almost brutish if not for his high cheekbones and lush lips. He's huge and built, and when I look at him, all I can remember is how those muscled arms felt wrapped around me.

"You're not supposed to leave the camp alone," he tells us, although his gaze seems to be glued to my face.

Irritation sweeps through me. Not for the first time, I long for my life on Earth. There, I'm a trauma nurse, charged with saving people's lives. Here, I'm not trusted to take a walk alone.

I sigh. There's a reason for that. The Dokhalls are still out there somewhere, likely regrouping. Staying within the camp is the smart choice until they're caught.

But I'm sick of them taking things from us. They took my health, my hope, and my freedom. And now they're doing it again.

I clear my throat. "You're right," I acknowledge. He looks

at me silently for a long moment, and the air seems to crackle between us.

"I'll walk you back," he finally says.

Vivian slides me a glance, raising one eyebrow. I shake my head at her. No, I don't know what the hell is happening between me and Tagiz.

All I know is he saved my life. It was his voice in my ear that gave me the strength to keep breathing when I was ready to give up.

And then I kissed him. And he told me he didn't want to *hurt* me.

Talk about a blow to my ego.

He reaches out to take my basket from me, and my hands tighten on it. He tilts his head, studying my face, and I release my hands, letting him take it.

I don't know what I have to do to make him see I'm not fragile.

"Hold on, little female. Just hold on. I won't let you die."

I glance at him and find his gaze still on my face as we all walk silently back toward camp.

* * *

Tagiz

I clench my teeth as I walk Zoey and her friends to the healers' kradi. She still has to take a healing tonic each day to fix the damage to her body. The reminder of how close she came to death makes me want to roar.

She studies me out of huge blue eyes. Her nose is covered in tiny brown freckles, highlighting its small shape. I spent hours counting those freckles while she was unconscious as I willed her to live.

Her lips are pink and plump, her top lip slightly larger than the bottom, and the feel of them against mine...

No, Tagiz. She is not for you.

The other females chat amongst themselves while Zoey walks silently through the forest, glancing at me occasionally. I know I hurt her that day, when she grinned up at me, full of innocence and good humor. She wrapped her hand around my neck, pulled my mouth to hers, and for a moment, the rest of the universe disappeared.

But sanity prevailed and I pulled away, attempting to ignore the dismay that entered those wide blue eyes.

Tiny, fragile human females are not for me. Especially *this* tiny, fragile human female.

I offer my hand to help Zoey over a large tree trunk, and she tilts her head. After a moment, she reaches for my hand, and it takes all my willpower to release her when she is safely over the fallen tree.

The camp is waking when we arrive. The sun has risen, and warriors are heading to the training arena. Sentries are coming off shift, while others replace them, and the smell of baking bread makes my stomach rumble as we walk past the main food kradi.

"Tagiz?"

I turn as Malis approaches. She looks tired, her face drawn, and she gazes at Zoey curiously.

I almost curse. I have such little time with Zoey these days. "What do you need?"

She blinks at my abrupt question, and her gaze flicks back to me. "Our parents would like us to meet them for breakfast," she murmurs.

Zoey is silent next to me, and a tug on my hand makes me glance down. She's pulling at her basket, and I release it abruptly. The sudden movement pushes her off-balance, but she recovers, her face flushing.

She nods at Malis and gives me one last glance before turning and walking into the healers' kradi.

"She is the human you rescued," Malis murmurs as we turn.

"I am only *one* of the people who were there for that mission," I say. Behind me, I hear a sharp indrawn breath from inside the kradi, followed by a choked cough. I tamp down my instinct to stalk into the kradi and demand why the little human is taking so long to recover.

I *know* why. Humans are much weaker than Braxians. Their bodies are not strong like ours.

Flashing blue eyes appear in my mind, burning with determination as the tiny human fought to live.

I push the memory away as Malis links her arm through mine.

"What are we going to do, Tagiz?"

I scowl at the thought of the meeting we will be having with our parents. "We must make them see that a mating between us is not the right choice."

Malis blinks back tears. "I love Heric. He makes me feel..."

"Alive," I finish for her with a sigh. "I know."

Heric is a quiet warrior. He's a good, capable fighter who can be trusted at any warrior's back. And yet he prefers learning to fighting. He can often be found discussing various herbs with the healers or mulling over the stars with the wisewomen. Rakiz also often asks his advice for battle strategy, as the warrior has an uncanny knack for predicting the movements of our enemies.

Malis has loved him since they were children. Soon after she learned to walk, one of the other children took her toy, taunting her with it. Heric took it back and stayed by her side for the rest of the day.

They've been inseparable ever since.

Unfortunately, our parents have other plans.

My father's kradi is bustling when we arrive. His years of loyalty to Rakiz's father served him well, and his home is large and comfortable. My mother is sitting in the small garden outside with Ornia—Malis's mother.

"My son," my mother says, getting to her feet. "It has been too long."

I smile at that. I saw her just a few nights ago for the evening meal. If my mother had her way, I would move back in with her and my father.

Along with the mate they picked for me before I could even hold a sword, of course.

Malis greets her mother, and Ornia nods at me. We take our seats, waiting for both our fathers. There is no question what this meeting is about. Both our families are tired of waiting.

They are here to urge us to mate.

Zoey

I choke down the tonic Moni insists I still need. Since the healer managed to use whatever passes as antibiotics on this planet to save my life, I trust her enough to come back each day and gag on her disgusting brown brew.

"How many more days of this?"

"Until I no longer hear you coughing at night, child."

I scowl at that. It took me weeks before the healers could be convinced I was able to move into my own kradi. And don't even get me started on Tagiz's objections. Finally, I went directly to Rakiz, who met with Moni. The result? My kradi is just a few kradis down from this one so Moni can keep an eye on me.

"I'm not saying dying is worse than drinking this tonic, but I'm not *not* saying that either," I mutter.

I hand the cup back to Moni, who turns to murmur to Sarissa. Vivian has already taken off, and I reach for the ingredients I need for the pain tonic I'll be making today.

Sarissa sits on one of the beds, her face intent as she chats to Moni. I get to work on a pain tonic, the task easy now, the repetition soothing. When I told Moni I was also a healer on my planet, she agreed to begin teaching me about healing on Agron. Sometimes, she makes me tell her about the technology we use in hospitals on Earth, her dark eyes wide. The healers here do incredibly well with what they have, but it's still a barbaric alien planet.

At the same time, I've seen miracles happen on Agron. Things I could never explain. The cava berries Arix's healers used when Dragix almost died are the stuff of legend.

And apparently, they're guarded as if they're gold.

I'm making the best of my life here. At least until we can get off this planet. But the truth is, I miss Earth so much that I still sometimes wake up, convinced I've slept through my alarm and I'm going to be late for my shift at the hospital.

I sometimes wonder what I would've done—if I'd known life as I knew it would be stolen from me. Maybe that's why it's better to have no warning. Every day, we get up and make plans based on the assumption we'll have years left of the same routine.

Oh, we know—in theory—we could die anytime. That something catastrophic could happen and shake us out of our normal lives. But our brains aren't designed to live with that fear. So we ignore it until it actually happens.

"Hand me the zavia, child."

I jolt, realizing I'm staring into space. I grab the salve and lean over, handing it to Moni. My gaze can't help but be drawn to where Sarissa has pulled up her dress, her calves on display.

Long, winding scars cover her lower legs, and I blink.

The corner of her mouth tips up as she watches me.

"Pretty gnarly, huh?"

"What happened?"

Her eyes turn wounded, her face paling, and I instantly regret asking. I open my mouth only to jump as one of Rakiz's warriors storms into the kradi.

"We need healers," he snaps. "The Dokhalls attempted to take their ship back. They took our warriors by surprise."

I jump into action, running for my own kradi. One of the first things I did when I was back on my feet was create a first aid kit. I haul it with me, joining Moni as the warriors hurry her along.

They don't argue when I reach Hewex, who is mounting one of the mishua.

"Tagiz won't like this," he mutters as he pulls me up in front of him.

"Save it," I snap, and he chuckles but turns the mishua toward the forest, urging her into a teeth-rattling gallop.

Relief is clear on the warriors' faces when we arrive. Rakiz is already there, holding one of his warrior's hands as the guy chokes on his own blood. Moni hurries toward them, and I scan the clearing. The trees are still burned-out husks after Dragix fought the Dokhalls here a few weeks ago. To the left, the ship is still standing, and it's evident these warriors guarded it with their lives.

Three of them are already dead, and my heart hurts at the sight. I push it away, focusing on what I can control right now. Five more warriors are injured, not counting the one Moni is treating. One of them is holding a blood-soaked shirt to his head, and I kneel in front of him, pressing two fingers to his neck. I attempt to ignore the frustration that rises. What I would give for a pulse oximeter or an EKG. Even a simple wristwatch would be handy.

His pulse isn't thready or irregular though, so I pull a skin of clean, boiled water from my first aid kit and irrigate his head wound.

"What's your name?" I murmur as he winces.

"Gravis."

"I'm Zoey."

"I know," he says.

He gives me a tiny smile and then winces again as I move his head slightly so I can get a better look as I check his pupils.

"What happened here?" I've heard about the attack already, of course, but I want to see if he's dealing with any confusion or forgetfulness.

"Dokhall bastards," he scowls. "Came out of nowhere. They must've been watching us for some time, waiting for their chance."

"Thank you for guarding our ship."

He smiles at me again, and I reach for the antiseptic paste Moni favors for these types of wounds.

"This will sting."

He takes it like a man, although his jaw clenches as I smooth the paste in place. The biggest worry on Agron is infection, although I sometimes wonder if the Braxians are less prone to infections compared to us humans. They seem to recover from wounds more quickly as well.

"It doesn't look like you'll need stitches," I tell him. "Hold this for me and I'll bandage you up."

He does as I ask, and I examine his face. "Any other injuries?"

He shakes his head, and I tie the bandage in place. "You'll need that changed. Come to the healers' kradi in a few hours or earlier if it bleeds through."

"Thank you."

I smile at him and turn to the next warrior, who has a deep slice in his shoulder.

"Zoey."

I turn at the sound of Tagiz's voice. His jaw is tight, and he looks displeased with me. Again.

I sigh. What else is new?

"How soon until we can move everyone back to the camp?" Tagiz asks.

I turn back to the warrior currently sitting with his back against a tree. His dark eyes are hazy with pain, but like all the Braxian warriors, he's silent and stoic.

"These guys are both okay to move, but I'm not sure about the others yet."

"We need to leave. Soon."

I glance back over my shoulder at Tagiz, but he's scanning our surroundings. He gestures to a few warriors, who move closer to Rakiz, and I get it.

He doesn't think we're safe here. And he's probably right.

I survey the warrior. He'll definitely need stitches, so I cover the wound with a thick bandage, wrapping it tight in the meantime.

"Any other injuries I need to know about?"

He shakes his head. "I took them down." He gestures toward a pile of purple bodies behind our blackened tree, and my stomach swims. I usually have a rock-solid stomach, but that was a massacre.

I glance away from the detached limbs and heads and turn to the remaining injured warriors. Rakiz lays his hand over a warrior's eyes, closing them as he breathes his last breath, and my throat aches at the look on Rakiz's face as he gets to his feet.

The other healers pronounce the remaining warriors good to go, and they're loaded onto the mishua. Hewex gestures for me to join Tagiz, and I narrow my eyes at him, but he ignores me, helping one of the injured warriors onto the mishua in front of him.

Tagiz is silent behind me. For about two minutes.

"I don't want you leaving the camp," he murmurs in my ear, and I almost shiver. "It's too dangerous."

"I'll take that under advisement," I say.

I can practically hear him grinding his teeth behind me.

"You're still healing."

"I'm almost completely recovered, Tagiz. I know you think I'm fragile, but I'm not."

"You're human."

The way he says *human* pisses me off, and I glower over my shoulder at him. "Braxians aren't exactly invincible, you know." I gesture at the mishua, who are being guided by stone-faced warriors making sure the bodies of their friends don't fall to the ground.

He's silent, but his arm around my waist clutches me closer to him.

"Stay with me, Zoey. You need to fight. Fight to live."

It's ironic, really. Because when he's around, I no longer feel like someone is sitting on my chest. I can...breathe.

Part of me wishes it had been anyone but Tagiz who helped rescue me that day. Because when someone sees you at your worst, it's hard to remove that memory from their minds. I'm pretty sure every time he looks at me, he sees me gasping for air and choking on mucus.

Sexy. Real sexy.

I firm my lips. I'm going to make him see me as a woman. And when he does, I'm going to make him *beg* for me.

CHAPTER TWO

Z oey

Nevada calls a meeting when I get back to camp. The warriors will be having their own meetings, but she acts as our intermediary, keeping us informed about everything we need to know. She also passes any important information on to Rakiz and negotiates with him when we want to do something the Braxians probably won't approve of.

Usually, we'd all file into one of the spare kradis. But with the new human women, we can't fit. So we meet in a small clearing instead. Nevada trained our sentries herself, so I know she takes this attack personally. Unfortunately, the Dokhalls are much smarter than the Voildi, and they're motivated by the fact we have their ship.

Our ship.

I sigh as I glance around the clearing. Sometimes I still have to pinch myself when I wake up to an emerald sky.

What would I have changed if I'd known I'd end up on this planet? What would I have done differently?

There's no point looking back. I know that now—after so many days in that cage, waiting to die. All I can do is look forward, even though I have no idea what my future will hold.

"How are you feeling?" I ask Nevada as she scans the clearing, her foot tapping impatiently as she waits for everyone to arrive.

"Like I have a brick sitting on my bladder," she murmurs.

I laugh, and she meets my eyes with a smile.

"Here." She grabs my hand and pulls it to her stomach, waiting a moment, and I grin at her as a tiny hand or foot makes contact with my palm.

"That's amazing. I'm so happy for you, Nevada."

By now, I'm close with all the human women I arrived here with. But I have a special bond with Nevada. She saved me when I was certain I was going to die. And she did it in style, blowing up the horrible building where I was being kept in that cage.

Of course, she didn't do it alone. Rakiz, Hewex, and Tagiz were there with her.

Just keep breathing, female. I'll get you out of here.

I shake off the memories, laughing as the baby kicks my hand again.

"Do you know when you're due?"

She shrugs. "Moni said it's not uncommon for Braxian babies to be born after four or five months. Since it's nine months for us humans, I'm guessing it'll be somewhere in between."

That explains the size of the bump. "Wow," I say. "I don't know if I'd be able to deal with the mystery of it all."

She snorts. "You're telling me. I'm attempting to be Zen about it, but it's not my best thing."

I laugh and leave her to wrangle the women as they arrive. I wave across the clearing to Maez, who's currently deep in conversation with a woman named Emma. She raises her hand with a grin, and I find a seat next to Ellie, who smiles as I plop down next to her. She's also pregnant, and I take her wrist, automatically pressing two fingers to her pulse. Her smile widens, but she's quiet as we watch everyone arrive.

"Where's Charlie?" I ask.

"She and Dragix are doing regular flyovers. Turns out, purple is easy to spot from up high. They're hunting any Dokhalls they see."

I smile at that. I never could've imagined dragons existed. Or that they turned into incredibly hot men.

Shows what I knew.

The clearing begins filling up as more of the new women arrive, and I study them.

The women were on the ship of Dokhalls, on their way to be taken back to the Dokhalls' planet after they had been bought at the slave market. Just like we were. It was their lucky day when the Dokhalls were sent to check out this planet instead. The Dokhalls were looking for their "products" that had escaped, and instead, many of them ended up dead.

But not all of them.

Sarissa leans back against one of the trees, her eyes serious as she watches everyone and everything. She managed to keep the other women from losing their minds when they first got free, and since then, she seems to have handed over leadership to a woman called Clara.

Clara immediately heads toward Nevada when she

arrives, and they murmur to each other for a moment. I feel a pang as I realize I've only spoken to Clara once. I've mostly been burying myself in the healers' kradi.

Alexis steps through the trees, and I jump to my feet, throwing my arms around her.

"What are you doing here? I thought you and Dexar were staying at camp?"

"We were until this attack. I've been examining the ship regularly, and Dexar lost his shit when he heard the Dokhalls killed Rakiz's men." She chews on her lip. "He says he won't let me go near any ship again until the Dokhall issue has been 'resolved.'"

Sarissa snorts from where she's still sitting against the tree. "Resolved. I like it."

Alexis grins at her. "Same." Her grin falls. "But I can't figure out our next step with this ship until we've handled the Dokhalls."

Sarissa nods and opens her mouth, but Nevada raises her hand, gesturing for everyone to shut up.

"Holy shit," Alexis murmurs. "Is she wearing a...dress?"

I laugh. "Yeah, there were only so many times she could adjust those leather pants."

Nevada can't possibly hear us across the clearing, but she glances over at us with a scowl, as if she knows exactly what we're talking about. Alexis gives her a finger wave, and Nevada glowers at her even as her mouth twitches.

Ellie is further along in her pregnancy, but the way Nevada is carrying makes her seem like she could have her baby any day. She looks healthy and strong, although she's rubbing her lower back as she surveys everyone in the clearing.

"Okay," Nevada says. "I misplaced my microphone, so y'all need to be quiet and wait for question time."

A few women chuckle at that.

She waits for the last few women to file in and then gets straight to the point.

"We need to take care of our little Dokhall problem. Rakiz and Dexar are currently meeting to figure out a plan. We had thought it was just the Dokhalls we needed to worry about, but there have been reports they may be allying with the Zintas."

A small blonde woman raises her hand, and Nevada nods at her.

"The Zintas?"

"Furry bastards from across the water. They come over here to trade occasionally, and they have no problem with buying slaves. They bit off more than they could chew when they took Ivy, and our honey-bunnies made them see the error of their ways. The problem is there are so many of them, and we also don't know how many Dokhalls escaped."

She frowns, staring off into space for a moment, and then seems to shake herself. "Based on how many you guys said were on the ship, there could still be hundreds of them out there. Combine that with the Zintas and we could be in trouble."

A voice speaks up from within the crowd. "They're not taking our fucking ship."

"Yeah," someone agrees. "Finders keepers."

Nevada nods. "They're not. You guys want off this planet, and we'll help you. As agreed. But you're going to have to buckle in for what could be a long ride. The ship is damaged, the Dokhalls are out for revenge, and the Zintas are a threat."

"Sure," someone else mutters, and I crane my head to see a woman with long dark hair braided back from her face. "But we have a motherfucking dragon."

Nevada grins at that. "We do. As far as weapons go, we can't get much better. The problem is the Zintas know how Dragix operates, and they're used to hiding their scent from him. If they're teaching our new purple friends the same tactics, Dragix may not be all that effective until he can actually *see* them."

The clearing goes quiet, and it's Beth who speaks, her cheeks coloring as heads turn toward her. I didn't notice her arrival, but she and Zarix must have traveled here with Alexis and Dexar.

"We need to set some kind of trap for them. Something that allows us to take them all out at once."

Nevada nods, and Kate gets to her feet, turning to Alexis.

"What can you tell us about the ship?" All eyes are on Kate, and I wonder if she realizes how much pressure she's going to be under if we *can* eventually get this ship off the ground. She was once a fighter pilot, and before the Arcav invaded, was working for a company attempting to send planes into space.

She seems cool and composed and exactly like the type of woman we'll need piloting our ship if we *can* get it working.

Alexis grins at Kate and moves toward the front of the group. I only knew Alexis for a few hours before I was kidnapped with Ivy and Beth, but her time on Agron has been good to her. She looks every inch the tribe queen, dressed in a long, gauzy purple dress with gold thread, her hair braided back off her face.

A breeze sweeps through the clearing, bringing the scent of meat cooking from the food kradi. My stomach rumbles.

"Okay," Alexis says. "I want to be clear with everyone before we get started. I'm an astronautical engineer. *On Earth.* So yes, that means I'm probably a better choice for attempting to fix this ship than say...Nevada." She grins, and Nevada snorts. "But attempting to understand how an alien ship works is like handing a Tesla to someone who has only ever worked on classic cars. It may have four wheels, but the technology is massively different. I'm working in the dark here. So I know you're pinning all your hopes on me figuring this out, and I get it. But you need to accept that even if I *can* fix this ship, there's a good chance I won't be able to find the materials to do that on this planet."

My heart sinks. "So our chances of actually using this ship aren't high."

"I've been traveling amongst this ship, the one we crash-landed here in, and the one that crashed here forty years ago. This has allowed me to compare some of the technology and try to understand what we're working with. The ship was set on fire in the last battle, and the fuselage is slightly cracked, but the damage is mostly cosmetic. So far, I know for sure one of the thrusters is broken."

Ellie raises her hand. "What is a thruster, and what does it do?"

"Thrusters help propel the ship into space. I don't know if the ship can operate properly without all the thrusters working, but I wouldn't risk it. The ship seems to run on artificial intelligence, which also isn't working. I'm 95 percent sure the AI system relies on a control chip. A chip that's currently missing." She sighs. "I think whichever Dokhall was responsible for landing that ship took the chip with him as insurance."

Silence.

Pale faces. And a few of the women have tears in their eyes. One of the women gets to her feet, the movement weary. "I've already decided to stay here," she announces. "But so many of us want to leave. We want the Grivath to pay for what they did to us. Are you saying without that chip, they can't get off this planet?"

Alexis chews on her lip. "At this stage, I'm not sure if you can operate the ship independently. It's possible those algorithms are used to change sequence as the ship is launching and operating and without it, it won't work." She holds up her hand as the clearing devolves into questions.

"Obviously, I'm going to try my best to help you guys get off Agron. But I want to be clear. If you get on this ship, you're risking your lives." She takes a moment, scanning each and every face as she lets that sink in. "If you stay on Agron, you can have a good life here. It may not be the life you imagined, but we sure like it. I understand the need for revenge, but you *have* to be sure this is what you want. Because even if I can get that ship launched, you'll be on your own after that."

Sarissa gets to her feet. "So you're saying at the very least, we need to fix the thruster. And you won't know more about whether or not we can use the ship without the chip until you've examined it, which you can't do until the Dokhalls are no longer a threat."

Alexis nods. "Pretty much."

"If they have that chip, they're not giving it up," someone calls out, and Sarissa nods, turning back to Alexis.

"Explain the broken thruster to me. Can we take it off the ship to repair it?"

Alexis shakes her head. "Not the whole thruster, but the part that's cracked can be removed."

Sarissa glances across the clearing to where Vivian is sitting, and they have a wordless conversation. Sarissa angles her head, and Vivian nods.

"After the battle, we talked about visiting Arix," Sarissa announces.

"Who's Arix?" one of the women pipes up.

"Arix is the king who helped save Dexar," Nevada says. "He offered to help us. Said he had people who 'tinker with metal and heat.'"

Sarissa nods. "I don't trust him. But then, I don't trust anyone."

Ellie frowns. "I don't really want us to be separated again. I want us to stay together."

I wrap my arm around her. Ellie is a sweetheart, a homebody, and she worries herself sick when we're away from camp.

Vivian bares her teeth in a fierce grin. "Well, I want to be closer to both a Sephora and a Starbucks, but as life has proven again and again on this planet, you can't always get what you want."

She winks as Ellie lets out a wet laugh. "If we take the thruster to him, maybe his people can help fix it while the Braxians handle the Dokhalls."

"Okay," Sarissa says. "We'll go to Arix."

"I'm going too." I feel my cheeks heat as everyone looks at me, but I ignore them. Vivian doesn't look surprised, giving me a nod.

"As long as Moni gives you the all clear." Nevada stares me down when I narrow my eyes at her, and I finally sigh.

"Yes, Mom."

She laughs, stroking her bump. "One thing is certain. No one leaves camp alone. We use the buddy system. We know these guys have weapons that can take us down. And we know they're more intelligent than the Voildi and much more organized than the Zintas. They're a threat that can't be ignored."

Tagiz

I survey the training arena, watching as the human females fight. According to Vrex, many of the new females have declared if they're going to be *temporarily* on Agron, they may as well train for their revenge.

Nevada stands in front of the group, hands on her hips. Rakiz glances over at her from where he is speaking with a group of his warriors, giving her a heated look, and she narrows her eyes, sending him a lewd gesture in return.

They both grin.

Something in my chest clenches. What would it be like to have that with someone? I have known Malis since we were children, but our parents' expectations have always been between us. In some ways, it's ironic. If not for their insistence we commit to mating, perhaps we would naturally have grown closer.

Now the only thing we have in common is loathing for the very thing our parents want so badly.

My father approaches, and I tense. He slides me a look and then returns his attention to the training arena. Some of the new human females are running from one end of the arena to the other while Nevada orders them to move faster.

"Weak human females," my father murmurs.

I glance at Ivy, Vrex's mate. She picks up a knife, which is more like a sword in her hand, and raises her eyebrow at her male, who is leaning against the training arena and talking to Terex.

Vrex smirks, jumps the arena fence, and stalks toward his mate.

"You have not seen these females fight as I have, Father. They may be small, but they can be vicious in battle."

He snorts. "They die too easily. And their children will

be weak. I am glad Rakiz's father cannot see the female his son has mated with. A tribe king has a duty to choose a Braxian female."

I grind my teeth. "Be careful, Father. If Rakiz hears you speak this way about his female..."

He shrugs but glances over his shoulder, checking our surroundings. For a moment, I feel sympathy for my mother. It's no secret their mating was not a love match. My father's family has been committed to "breeding strong and true" for centuries. The strongest females in the tribe are chosen, along with those who can form ongoing alliances with our own family.

My mother has never said she regrets mating with my father. Has never hinted this may be the case. And she agrees with him that I should mate with Malis. But I wonder, when she sees her friends, when she watches how they are adored by their mates...

Does she wish for more?

I shake my head at the thought. This is the future she wants for me. The future both my parents wish for me to have.

"I'm pleased you have no intention of choosing one of these weak human females," my father says. "Malis will be a good mate."

I don't want Malis. I long for the tiny, mouthy female who survived against all odds. The female with bright-blue eyes who challenges me at every turn.

I glance at my father, noting his eyes are on my face, searching for any hint of weakness.

I ensure my face is carefully blank. "We've spoken about this, Father. I have no intention of mating with *anyone* right now."

He narrows his eyes at me, and my stomach churns.

Beneath our every interaction is an unyielding thread of obligation. I owe my father more than I can ever repay. I owe him *everything.*

He nods at whatever he sees on my face and then points at Nevada. "Human females were not created to breed with us," he says quietly. "Rakiz hovers around his queen because he knows the truth. The likelihood of her dying in child-birth is high. I know you would not want to sentence a female to the same fate, Tagiz."

He slaps me on the shoulder, turning to walk away, and I stare at Nevada. At the large mound of her stomach.

A vision intrudes before I can stop it. Zoey, her face twisted in pain. But this time, instead of coughing, she is writhing, attempting to birth a Braxian baby that is far too big for her tiny body to handle.

I see her eyes fluttering shut for the last time. Because of my selfishness.

Jozet approaches from my left, a few steps away. From the look on his face, he was listening to every word my father said.

"Do you think that's true?" he asks. "Do you believe the queen will die attempting to bring the baby into the world?"

I'm silent, and he blows out a breath as we both return our attention to the arena.

Nevada winces, stroking her hand over her stomach, and Rakiz breaks off his conversation, immediately stalking to her. She smiles up at him, brushing a hand over his jaw, but now I can see the terror in his eyes.

And I understand it.

CHAPTER THREE

Z oey

I hand my first aid kit to Hewex, waiting while he attaches it to the mishua's saddle, and then I give him my bag. I haven't packed much—just a change of clothes in case we need to make camp. Vivian has the broken piece of the thruster, while Sarissa has a sketch and a list of instructions from Alexis.

Jozet helps Sarissa onto his mishua, and I take a moment to smile up at the green sky. Other than my constant trips to the forest, this is my first time leaving the camp since I was brought here, unconscious and barely breathing.

Unlike almost everyone else, I've never seen any of the other tribes. I was taken by the Voildi, carried to Sebe, and shoved into a cage.

But today, I'm going on a Braxian boat, across the lake or sea they call the Colossal Water, and I'm even going to see

the mysterious king everyone talks about in hushed whispers. According to Vivian, he lives in an actual *castle*.

If this weren't such an important trip, I'd probably be
doing a little victory dance.

"Take that, you purple bastards. You couldn't hold me
down."

"What was that?" Sarissa asks from her spot on Jozet's
mishua.

"Nothing."

She pushes her hair out of her eyes, then turns her
head, facing into the wind as she pulls it up into a ponytail. I raise my eyebrow at her elastic hair band, and she
notices me looking. "I had it around my wrist when I was
taken."

"Guard it like gold," I advise her, and she laughs.

"There are like forty women here and approximately ten
hair bands between us. Blaire's snapped the other day, and I
thought she was going to cry."

I grin. Blaire is tough as nails. She's small and fine-
boned, which according to her, comes from her Japanese
mother. But I've never seen her look anything other than
coolly amused.

I glance at Hewex. "Let's get this show on the road."

He sends me a shit-eating grin, and the expression is so
out of place on his craggy face that I blink at him.

"We're waiting for one more person," he says. Then he
glances over my shoulder, and that grin widens.

I close my eyes. I don't need to guess who is standing
behind me.

"Laugh it up," I mutter as Hewex chuckles. "You're on my
shit list now. It's not a good place to be."

I open my eyes as he has the nerve to pat me on the
head.

"That's it," I say. "That thing we talked about? It's happening now. You owe me."

"What thing?" a deep voice rumbles behind me.

I ignore that, and Tagiz steps into my space as Hewex helps Vivian onto his mishua.

I turn, taking a step back. I don't need to be close enough to smell the heady leather-and-male scent of the man who drives me crazy.

"None of your business. What are you doing here?"

"What do you think?"

"Don't answer a question with a question."

He grins at me, and I roll my eyes.

All amusement leaves his expression as he runs his gaze over my body. Unfortunately, it's not a sexy look. Instead, I can almost hear him wondering if I'm healthy enough to travel.

I turn away. "I'm not riding with him," I announce.

I yelp as the world turns upside down, and I smack him on the chest as he stalks to his mishua with me in his arms.

"Ooh, you are in *big* trouble, mister. Huge." I'm clenching my teeth, but the jerk doesn't seem at all worried. He ignores me, climbing up onto his mishua with me still in his arms. He helps me turn until I can throw my other leg over the side of the mishua, and I attempt to block out just how good his arm feels as he wraps it around my waist.

For the second time in three days, I'm sitting between Tagiz's thighs.

"Did you bring your tonic?" he murmurs in my ear, and all sexy thoughts flee from my head.

"I don't need it anymore," I grind out, teeth clenched in annoyance. He leans forward, taking my chin in his hand as he turns my head to face him. His expression is no longer amused.

"Zoey—"

That's it.

"You listen to me," I snap. "I'm an adult woman who *saves lives* on my planet. I'm responsible for my own health, and I've been following Moni's treatment plan. *You* have nothing to do with that plan. I'm not going to discuss this again, so if you don't have anything to talk to me about that doesn't involve my health, I suggest you don't say anything at all."

His eyes widen slightly as he examines my face. Whatever he sees must convince him I'm one-hundred-percent serious because his jaw tightens, but he nods, releasing my chin. I blink back tears as I make eye contact with Hewex, and he gives me a sympathetic look.

With a nod from him, we're on the move.

Tagiz

"Zoey."

She ignores me, and I sigh. "I...apologize."

She ignores that too, and I stare at the back of her head. Zoey is quick to laugh, and I have never seen her hold a grudge. I push down the panic that begins to rise at the thought of her no longer speaking to me.

When she was recovering from her illness, we would spend long nights talking. She told me of her work as a healer on Earth, and I explained how I grew up with Rakiz, certain I would continue my family's tradition and become one of his most loyal and trustworthy warriors.

I miss those nights with her.

Regret washes over me as I study the beautiful female

who is busy ignoring me. She turns her head slightly as Hewex says something, and I ignore the jealousy that stabs into me when she gives him a tiny smile.

She never smiles at me anymore.

"Zoey," I murmur again.

She stiffens. "What?" she finally says, and a surprising warmth in my chest makes me want to pull her even closer.

Zoey is the only female who has ever made me feel tenderness.

"Please accept my apology," I murmur. "I know I am... protective. It is only because I care about you."

She's silent for a long moment. "You may not see me as a woman, Tagiz, but I won't have you treating me like a child."

My mouth twists. "You were so sick..."

"And you'll never get past it. I understand, Tagiz," she says, and her voice is hollow. "But I won't allow you to interfere in my life."

I grind my teeth. I don't know how this happened. How I put that sadness in Zoey's voice. But I will fix it.

"I see you as an exquisite female, Zoey. You...dazzle me. If you can't see that, you haven't been paying attention."

I lean forward and whisper the last few words in her ear, and she shivers, glancing over her shoulder at me, those big blue eyes wider than ever.

"Don't play with my feelings, Tagiz."

I sigh. I should let her go. Let her find another warrior who will walk through the forest with her before dawn. Who will murmur with her at night and show her all the ways a Braxian can make a human female scream with pleasure?

The thought makes me clench my fists, and Zoey taps on my arm as it tightens around her waist.

I lean forward and murmur in her ear again. "Did I ever

tell you what I thought the first time I saw you open your eyes?"

Zoey laughs but not like the question is funny. "I give this weak human female two days before she's dead?"

I growl at that, leaning forward and nipping gently at her earlobe. I'm rewarded with her low groan, and she clutches my arm tighter as I murmur into her ear.

"I looked into your eyes, and all I could think was 'finally, I found her.' But you were so sick. The Voildi and the Zintas almost took you from me before I could even find you."

"If that's how you feel, then why wouldn't you kiss me?"

I open my mouth to attempt to explain, but Hewex pulls his mishua to a stop, and Jozet does the same.

"From here, we move fast," Hewex says in a low voice. "This is the perfect place for an attack, so we will not be lingering in this area."

We all nod, and my mishua needs no encouragement when Hewex directs us to gallop across the open clearing. She snorts, throwing her head in glee before sprinting after Hewex's mishua at a pace that makes Zoey clutch even tighter at the arm I have wrapped around her tiny waist.

As if I would ever allow her to be harmed. I scowl at the thought.

I continually scan our surroundings, aware everyone else is doing the same. The Dokhalls don't appear to be lying in wait; however, they may be waiting closer to the Colossal Water or perhaps planning to attack us when we return.

Who knows what these strange purple creatures have planned? All I know is we will slaughter each and every one of them before we allow them to take the human females from us.

Zoey

The trip across the water will only take a few hours, but the sound of Hewex's retching makes it feel longer. The poor guy pukes again and again, and Vivian wrinkles her nose at the sound as she offers him a cloth to wipe his face.

Tagiz murmurs something to him at one point, and Hewex scowls, his expression deadly before he turns away to hurl once more.

"What did you say to him?" I ask when Tagiz sits back down beside me.

"I told him he should have learned from the last time he crossed the Colossal Water."

Hewex wipes his mouth, his face pale and sweaty, and I feel for the guy. I wish I had some anti-nausea meds or something to give him so he could have some relief.

Earlier, Vivian warned me not to get too close to the edge of the boat. Yalex—our captain—nodded his head in agreement. "There are many different beasts waiting beneath the surface," he murmured, his eyes on the horizon. "You would likely be nothing but a snack."

I planted myself firmly in the middle of the boat, and now I'm keeping a close eye on Hewex as he loses his breakfast over the side.

Vivian and Sarissa are murmuring to each other as we approach the town, and I tamp down the jealousy that rises as they laugh.

I always wished for a sibling or a cousin, but I'm an only child. Mom came from money, but her parents disowned her when she fell for a man she later learned was married. When he abandoned us, she refused to give them the pleasure of saying "I told you so." Instead, she worked three jobs only to be struck by a drunk driver when she was crossing the street for her night shift at the diner. I was nineteen.

"What are you thinking?"

I glance at Tagiz, his words still on repeat in my mind.

"I looked into your eyes, and all I could think was 'finally, I found her.'"

If that's true, why doesn't he want me and only me?

I bet Mom wondered the same damn thing.

The thought makes my chest ache. Am I just repeating history?

I turn back at Sarissa and Vivian, who have their blonde heads so close together they're almost touching as they read over the information Alexis gave them.

"I'm feeling a little jealous," I admit. "I always wished I had siblings. I'd give anything to have family on this planet. Or someone I was friends with on Earth."

Tagiz studies me. "What about the other human females?"

I smile. "They're great, don't get me wrong. Nevada saved my life, and Ivy was the one who gave me the strength to get through that lonely time in the cage without her. But...I've been stuck in the healers' kradi while everyone else has been actually making a difference. It's hard not to feel a little left out sometimes."

Tagiz narrows his eyes at me, and I smile.

"It's okay. It'll come with time."

"Is that why you insist on doing these things? Coming across the Colossal Water and leaving the safety of the camp after an attack?"

I scowl at him, but for once he's not attempting to convince me to stay behind. He seems genuinely curious.

"I've always been someone who couldn't stand to see

people in pain. It sometimes felt like *I* was the one physically hurting when I was a kid. I managed to get control of that when I was studying, but I'm still driven to help. I believe I was given a gift. I'm calm under pressure. I don't fall apart. And I can multitask better than most people. They're all skills that are in high demand for nursing—especially trauma nursing. I can't leave people to suffer when I know I can help, Tagiz. It's not in me."

Tagiz leans forward, tucking a strand of hair behind my ear. "I...understand. Asking you not to help is like asking me not to fight. You feel it is your calling."

I nod, and he sits back, studying me.

"But what about this trip?"

I scan his face for judgment or annoyance, but he still seems genuinely curious.

"I'm *also* not the kind of person who is happy just sitting behind. I want these guys to pay. I want the Grivath to pay for abducting us, I want the Dokhalls to pay for buying us—and for breaking my ribs—and I want the Zintas to pay for working with them." I shrug. "I'm not used to feeling this way. Like I want to see someone *suffer*. And maybe when it comes down to it, I won't be able to witness it. But for now, I think I should get to make that decision for myself and choose what I feel I can handle. Don't you?"

The question is more rhetorical than anything else, but Tagiz angles his head. This is something I love about him. When I'm with him, he gives me 100 percent of his attention. He doesn't ever provide flippant answers or brush me off. If I ask him a question, even something simple, he always gives the answer careful consideration.

"Yes," he says finally, and to my surprise, he throws his arm around my shoulders and pulls me close. "I do."

I give in to my instincts and snuggle close, inhaling his

warm, masculine scent. Within a few minutes, we're almost at the shore, and Yalex gives orders as we dock.

We leave him with the boat, and I turn, surveying the town.

I've heard all about it, of course. In fact, I've made Vivian, Ivy, and Charlie all tell me every detail they could... multiple times.

But still, I was somehow unprepared to see an actual town.

"Pretty amazing, huh?" Vivian smiles at me.

"That's one word for it." I've spent so much time in the camp that the sights, sounds, and smells of this place feel like an assault.

And yet I feel like I could stand here on this dock for hours. Just...watching.

Fishermen are bringing in nets of fish along with a few other creatures, one of which has gold scales and huge teeth and looks like a cross between an octopus and a shark. I shudder, turning my attention to the busy cobbled street in front of us.

Tagiz, Jozet, and Hewex seem to know where they're going, surrounding us as we walk together. The buildings are so close together they remind me of photos I've seen of Amsterdam. While many of them seem shabby and worn, several are multiple stories high.

I stop and stare up at a collection of bright flower boxes on a balcony. A woman with gray skin and bright-orange hair is watering her flowers, and she raises one eyebrow as our gazes meet.

I smile at her and glance away. Great, now I'm the weird creeper staring at people who are just going about their business.

Tagiz takes my elbow as I almost walk into a guy carrying a cage full of animals that look similar to chickens. He must be eight or nine feet tall, and his long arms wrap around the huge cage, making it look effortless.

"Zoey." Tagiz's voice is amused as I stumble. "Pay attention."

I grin at him. "I can't help it. You've been here before. I barely got to travel on Earth." I've only been to Canada once with Mom before she died. "This is like something out of a movie."

Tagiz's dark eyes search my face. "I don't know what a movie is, but I am...glad you are enjoying yourself."

He tucks me close and acts as my shield, keeping me on the right path while preventing me from running into anyone.

I can smell some kind of nuts roasting, and a vendor calls out to us as we walk past, shaking a bag at me. Tagiz takes one look at my face and gestures to Hewex to stand close while he hands over a couple of coins before bringing the bag to us.

"Mmm," Vivian says as we pass the bag amongst the three of us. "They're spicy and sweet at the same time."

While we're acting like we're wandering the streets of Europe, the warriors are examining anyone who gets too close.

"Okay." Sarissa nods as we convince the warriors to let us examine a table holding gleaming silver knives. "I'm still not happy about the whole alien abduction thing, but I'm glad I'll at least be able to tell my grandchildren about this place one day."

Vivian elbows her. "Told you," she says, and they both crack up. I smile, but my attention is currently focused on the four Braxians walking toward us. They're dressed entirely in black and gold, and they seem more...groomed than the Braxians we see every day.

"We received word you had arrived," one of them tells Tagiz. "We have been instructed to take you to the king."

Ooh.

I know nothing about Arix—except that when Dragix almost died, and Charlie was falling apart in front of our eyes, Arix's healers managed to save his life. They used something they called cava berries, and Moni's eyes lit up when she was told about them.

I'm itching to learn more about them.

The one and only time I saw Arix was when we were in the healers' kradi after the battle. Vivian and Dragix were recovering, and Arix offered his city as a place we could find help to fix our ship. Here's my problem with that: we know nothing about the guy. He's been ruling his territory on this planet this entire time, and yet the Braxians only just heard of him, the first time they made it across the water.

Plus, the way he looked at Vivian made it clear he wouldn't be helping us out of the goodness of his heart.

The guards are still waiting, and I can't help but examine their coal-black uniforms with the shiny bright-gold buttons and polished boots and the swords on their hips, the handles gleaming in the sun. They look nothing like the Braxians on our side of the water.

One of them runs his gaze over us all curiously, and then they murmur amongst themselves before leading us further down the street and to the right.

I gasp. If I thought the dock and the streets leading here were exciting, they have nothing on the castle. The first time I heard about this place, I made the other women tell me everything, describing it over and over. But nothing could have prepared me for the gleaming obsidian castle, its huge spires shooting into the sky in the distance.

The sight of it makes me shiver, and I'm once again reminded of how little I know about this planet. I thought it was all as undeveloped as our side of Agron. But if this medieval-looking town is just a few hours away by boat, could there be an even bigger city on another continent?

The guards have been waiting patiently for us as we stared down the hill at the castle. We follow them down the long street, and within a few minutes, we're walking through wide black doors.

The temperature is much cooler in here. Sarissa surveys the huge entrance hall and then practically presses her nose against one of the walls as she examines the silver threads running through the black stone.

I glance up. And up. And up. High above us, as if suspended in the air, a network of corridors weave around one another like silver scarves. A long staircase leads up to those corridors, the white steps contrasting sharply with the black walls.

It feels like a cathedral, with the hushed silence that reminds me of a museum on Earth.

"This way," one of the guards says, gesturing to the left, and we follow him through the doors to a throne room.

Natural light fills the space, pouring in from the huge windows on both sides of the large room. It's empty, save for the Braxian king who sits on a polished black throne and another Braxian with burning silver eyes and a face like stone who stands beside him.

Arix doesn't look at all surprised to see us. But he does look...pleased. In fact, his expression is perilously close to smug as his gaze slides past me and Sarissa and lands on Vivian.

"Hello, lovely," he purrs.

CHAPTER FOUR

Z oey

Vivian stares at Arix, and trepidation, interest, and curiosity all cross her face before she settles on indifference.

But I know Vivian, and I can tell by the way her hand is smoothing her dress that she's nervous.

I thought I would let her do the talking; after all, she's the only one of us Arix seems to tolerate. But she's clamming up, her gaze darting around the throne room.

I've never seen self-assured, controlled Vivian like this before. It's like we're in some kind of twilight zone. Sarissa obviously feels the same because she shoots her cousin a wide-eyed look before turning to address the king.

"When you came to Rakiz's camp, you offered to help us fix our ship."

He nods. "The offer still stands."

The Braxian by his side shifts in obvious disapproval but keeps his mouth shut as he runs his eyes over each of us.

I glance at Hewex, and he pulls the cone-shaped device out of the canvas bag he's carrying. Vivian takes it, and Arix watches her as she steps forward, displaying it to him. It reminds me of one of those plastic cones we put around our pets' necks on Earth when we've had them fixed. Only, it's made out of some kind of metal, and it has a long crack up one side.

"This is a piece of one of our thrusters," Vivian says. "As you can see, it needs to be fixed."

Arix nods. "There are many metalsmiths who can help you with this. If it can't be fixed, they may be able to replace it."

"There's something else." Vivian's tone is hesitant, and Arix's eyes narrow as he gazes at her. I glance at Sarissa, but her attention is completely focused on Arix as if waiting for him to make some kind of move.

"Yes?"

"The Dokhalls took a control chip that we likely need to run our ship. None of us have piloted a spaceship before, so we're relying on an artificially intelligent system to do the heavy lifting for us. Without that chip, we may not get off the ground."

Arix nods, his expression thoughtful. "I can't promise you will be able to find a replacement for this chip, but perhaps..."

He gets to his feet, and I almost gasp. God, he's huge.

"If you would like to come with me, I will show you the most likely place to find such a thing."

The Braxian next to him growls something under this breath, and Arix grins.

"My commander is unhappy at this idea," he murmurs. The commander gives Arix a look, and his grin widens.

Sarissa narrows her eyes at the commander, obviously deciding he's also a threat.

I glance at Tagiz, who's currently stone-faced, but he's letting us choose whether we'll follow Arix.

Vivian turns to Sarissa, who shrugs, and then tilts her head as she looks at me.

I consider it. I don't trust this Braxian. I'm sure he has his own motives for helping us, and whatever those motives are, I'm committed to figuring them out. But he hasn't threatened us or hurt us so far. And if he can help...

I nod, and Vivian turns back to Arix, who looks amused at our silent discussion.

"Please, show us."

He strides down the steps leading to his throne and offers his arm to Vivian. The commander chooses to stay behind, but he gives each of us a burning look, which Sarissa returns.

Tagiz, Hewex, and Jozet are all tense, but we follow the king out of the throne room, where a group of guards instantly surrounds us.

Tagiz snarls at one of the guards as he gets too close to me, and Arix glances over his shoulder. His expression is mild, but the guard instantly bows his head, backing up to give us space.

We all walk back into the huge entrance hall, only this time, Arix leads us behind the staircase to another corridor. We traipse along behind him, and I can tell by the expression on Tagiz's face that he doesn't like this one bit.

"If anything happens, I want you to run back to the boat," he murmurs into my ear as we walk along gleaming silver tiles. "Don't hesitate. Just get back to Yalex."

I slide him a look. "You think I'd leave you here? That's cute."

His jaw tightens at that, and he opens his mouth—likely to make another ridiculous suggestion—but one of Arix's guards opens the black door in front of us, and I'm suddenly blinking into the sunlight.

We must be behind the castle, and we file down black stone steps onto the grass. In front of us is a small, private dock where I count twelve tiny boats. They look almost like the gondolas I've seen in pictures of Venice, except they seem slightly wider.

The warriors aren't exactly pleased by this, which isn't surprising, since most Braxians can't swim.

Vivian glances back at me for reassurance as we step back onto the dock, and I nod. Arix is playing his own game, and I'm not sure what that game is. But that doesn't mean we can't win our own game. If he can help us get off this planet, we'd be idiots not to take his help.

We're all silent as more guards step forward, readying the gondolas. "What are these called?" I ask a guard, and he grunts.

"Hydros," he says.

The guard holds out his hand to help me into the hydro, but Tagiz is suddenly there, shooting him an unfriendly look. I'm grateful for Tagiz's hand as I maneuver my dress, hoping I don't face-plant as I climb rather ungracefully into the tiny boat. Tagiz sits beside me, and I watch as Hewex and Sarissa get settled as well. Arix is helping Vivian into their own hydro, and he shakes his head as Jozet attempts to board with them.

Vivian sends Jozet a reassuring look. He doesn't seem happy but moves toward our hydro instead.

For whatever reason, Arix wants Vivian to himself. It's obvious he's attracted to her, but I didn't expect to see Vivian's reaction to him. She's as unsure as I've ever seen her, a blush creeping up her cheeks as Arix leans over and murmurs something to her.

His guards pile into their own hydros.

"Where do you think he's taking us?" I ask, and Tagiz shrugs. His eyes are continually scanning everything around us as the guards begin to direct the hydros down the river.

Other than the gentle splash of water, it's quiet. Peaceful. The sun is warm on my face, and I lean against Tagiz for a moment. He glances down at me and wraps his arm around me again.

The river flows through this town, and my head turns continually as I attempt to take everything in. On one side of the river, small, thatched houses sit next to each other on each side of a cobbled street. Mishua are either ridden by Braxians or attached to carts, some of which are stopping in front of houses to make deliveries.

We travel beneath bridges, which connect one side of the town to the other. Eventually, the houses become more and more sparse and are replaced by trees. We must go downriver for at least half an hour before we stop at another dock, this one much smaller than the one at the castle.

We're in the middle of nowhere.

Vivian doesn't look concerned, although she's got that blank expression on her face that tells me she's worried but attempting to hide it. Arix helps her from the hydro, and we all file onto the dock.

"Where are we?" Sarissa asks.

Arix smiles. "You will soon see."

Sarissa frowns, likely about to demand more information, but he's already turning away, offering Vivian his arm. Sarissa glances over her shoulder at me.

"I really hate this," she mutters, and I nod.

"Same. But this is Arix's little party. We're just the entertainment."

She scowls at that, but we trail after the king, who doesn't look at all concerned by our hesitation. Tagiz is no longer even pretending to be okay with this, and his sword is now in his hand, which explains why Arix's guards are huddling even closer around us, their hands hovering over their own swords.

I blow out a breath, my senses heightened. I'm keeping my eyes on the king as we walk along a cobbled path leading into a thicket of trees. The trees tower over us, their thick limbs a dense canopy that only allows occasional glimpses at the sky.

Sarissa sidles closer to me, her eyes hard. "What do you think is going on?" she murmurs.

"I have no idea. Arix seems to enjoy the mystery of it all."

We must walk for another ten minutes. The musty scent of moss is heavy in the air, and it's eerily quiet. It's as if even the animals who make this part of the forest their home are wary of the Braxian king, who strolls through their territory with a look of cool amusement on his face.

The trees begin to thin, and we all freeze.

"What is this?" Vivian asks.

Arix glances at her before returning his attention to the bustling market that stretches in front of us.

"This," he says, "is the marketplace."

He says "marketplace" as if it should be capitalized.

"The marketplace?" I ask, and he nods.

"While Agron may not be as developed as many other planets in this galaxy, we are not without our contacts. There are a few vendors brave enough to take the journey here, bringing goods and services for trade."

The trees are much sparser now, surrounding the large

clearing, which helps keep it hidden from prying eyes. I never could've imagined this place was here, and once again I find myself almost overwhelmed by how little I know about this planet.

On Earth, I knew that there were 197 countries. Here, I don't even know how many continents there are. It's both exciting and intimidating to know so little about a place where I'm likely to live for at least the short term.

There must be a hundred kradis set up in the space. Although, unlike the kradis back at our camp, these are three-sided, allowing vendors to protect their goods from the weather while negotiating with buyers.

A few weeks ago, Nevada told me about the market she visited with Rakiz when she was looking for me and Ivy. Her eyes sparkled as she described all the different types of aliens she saw, and she grinned as she told me all about the people who were trading with each other.

Now I can see why. There are people of all colors of the rainbow here, from purple to blue, green to yellow. Some have more than two arms; others have scales and fur. It's difficult not to stare.

Arix steps forward, and the entire market goes so quiet; I can hear a branch as it falls from a tree behind us. He waves his hand, his expression sardonic.

"Carry on," he says, and everyone gets back to business, haggling over food, jewelry, and weapons.

We must look like curious schoolchildren as we follow Arix through the stalls. People stare at the king, but for the most part, they ignore us. Arix seems to have a destination in mind, and he eventually stops at a kradi manned by two Braxian women.

One of them bows her head. "Yes, Your Majesty?"

Arix turns to Vivian, who holds up the broken part, and

the woman stretches out her hand to take it from her, her gray eyes curious.

"This is from an S23 thruster," she murmurs. "How did you get this?"

Arix raises one eyebrow at the woman, and she decides she doesn't need to ask any further questions.

"We can fix it, but these parts are so fragile that you risk another crack. If it cracks in flight, it can lead to a system overload, so I wouldn't risk it."

I stare at her, entranced by the way she talks about a spaceship as if discussing the weather.

"Do you have something we can use as a replacement part?" I ask.

The woman shakes her head, and my heart sinks, but her friend steps forward.

"We can order one in, but the shipment won't be arriving for weeks."

"The shipment?" Vivian asks, and Arix smiles down at her.

"Many of these vendors travel from trading posts on hub planets. Agron may be uncivilized compared to most, but our jewels and other goods are still in demand, mostly due to their rarity."

Vivian chews on her lip and glances at me.

I clear my throat. "How much will it cost?"

"Our contact prefers to negotiate in person," the woman says.

I nod. "Do you know when your contact will return so we'll know when we need to be back here?"

She shakes her head. "He has no true schedule. It depends on how his trading is going on other planets and if one of his buyers requests something only found on Agron."

Arix nods and takes Vivian's arm again, the movement

possessive. He leads us over to the trees, lowering his voice. "This market meets every few days," he says. "If you want to guarantee you will be here when the vendor arrives, you will need to ensure you are in the area. I am willing to help you find whatever parts you need if you would like to stay here."

And his game becomes clear. Vivian narrows her eyes at him. "I don't understand you."

He laughs. "You don't need to."

"Why do you want me here?"

"Am I not allowed to want to enjoy the pleasure of your company?"

"What's your endgame?"

"If I told you that, it would spoil the surprise," he purrs, and Vivian tilts her head as she studies him.

Then she turns back to us. "I'm staying."

I blink, and she gives me a tiny smile at whatever she sees on my face.

"Then I'm staying too," Sarissa says. Arix nods, seemingly unconcerned he may end up cockblocked by Vivian's cousin. I suppress a smile at the thought. Something tells me the king has more than enough ways to get around Sarissa if he needs to.

"Are you guys sure?" This has happened so suddenly it feels like the world is spinning out of control.

Vivian steps forward, taking my hands in hers. "This is my chance to contribute to us getting off this planet," she murmurs. "I'll be fine. I promise."

Next to us, Arix is very still. I study him, and his gaze shifts briefly to me. He raises an eyebrow and then returns his attention to Vivian.

I don't trust him as far as I can throw him, but ultimately, it's Vivian's decision. And I feel much better about the situation knowing Sarissa will be here as well.

I glance at Sarissa, whose face is carefully blank. Why *is* this guy so keen to help us? If he wants Vivian, helping us leave this planet is not the way to get what he wants.

"It's settled, then," Arix says, and I shiver at the pure triumph in his eyes.

———

Tagiz

Zoey is quiet on the trip back across the Colossal Water. It's evident she is unhappy to be leaving her friends behind.

"They will be safe," I say, and she glances at me, wincing as Hewex retches over the side of the boat.

"Arix is scary."

"He definitely wants Vivian, but I don't believe he will hurt her."

"He knows we're planning to fix our ship and she intends to leave this planet. Why would he help make that happen?"

I shrug. "Perhaps he is hoping he can convince her to stay."

She laughs at that. "Vivian is the least likely of all of us to stay here. Since the moment we landed, she has been one-hundred-percent focused on getting off this planet. What if he doesn't let her leave?"

"We will deal with that if it happens."

She searches my face and finally nods. By now, she knows our tribe will fight for the human females' freedom.

Silence stretches between us, but I can't help myself—I have to ask.

"And you? Do you plan to leave Agron?"

She glances at me, her blue eyes huge, and then she returns her attention to the water.

"Yes," she says, and my chest aches. "Unless someone gives me a reason to stay."

I should be happy for her. I should be pleased she will no longer be around. That I'll no longer be tempted by the kind, stubborn, beautiful female who makes my gut clench with *want*.

Instead, all I can think about is the male she will meet on her planet. The one she will gift with her wide smiles and soft touches. The one who will get to hear her bright laughter and soft moans.

The one who will kiss her, will stroke his tongue inside her mouth, strip off her clothes, and—

"Tagiz?"

Zoey glances up at me, wide-eyed, and I realize I'm shaking, my hands fisted.

"Uh, is everything okay?"

I nod, but I can't bring myself to speak of my thoughts. I want Zoey to have a good life. The kind of life she has always wanted. And it will be another male who will sleep next to her each night. Who will watch her belly grow rounded with his babe.

"Okay, Tagiz, seriously, what's wrong?"

"Nothing, little healer," I lie. She doesn't look convinced, but I will not voice my thoughts.

She raises one eyebrow. "Can I ask you something?"

"Of course."

"Are you going to mate with Malis?"

I shift, uncomfortable—both at the question and at the thought.

"It is...complicated."

"Uh-huh."

Zoey chooses not to ask any further questions, shrugging out from beneath my arm. "I'm going to go check on Hewex," she mutters.

I watch her go, my heart heavy, my body filled with regret.

CHAPTER FIVE

Z oey

"Are you listening, child?"

"Hmm?"

I blink, focusing on Moni, who looks amused. The healers' kradi is quiet at this time of the day, and we're currently taking stock of the most important salves and tonics.

"Sorry." I blush. My mind is a million miles away, all thoughts focused on one gorgeous, frustrating Braxian warrior. A warrior who is probably going to mate with someone else. The dickhead.

"What did you say?"

Moni raises one eyebrow but chooses not to comment. Yes, I've been distracted lately. But some nights, I'm lucky if I get just a few hours of sleep. And when I'm not gasping through my nightmares, I'm daydreaming about Tagiz.

"We need more maradoza berries," Moni says. "I would like to make more yaroz today."

I nod. Yaroz is a tonic and the closest thing Braxians have to a general anesthetic. Maradoza is the key ingredient, and the juice from the maradoza berries provide most of the properties that will knock someone out—during even the worst pain. But the measurements must be perfect during the creation of the tonic. Too much maradoza and the patient may not wake up. Not enough and they'll be able to feel everything.

I wipe my hands on my apron and remove it before plucking a small knife from one of the tables and shoving it in my pocket. It's so dull it's unlikely to cut through my dress, but it's helpful when I'm collecting specific herbs and plants.

"Anything else?"

"We need more ortar as well."

"Okay, no problem."

I know the rules, and I head to the training arena on my way to the forest. Hewex has just finished and is leaning against the fence, face flushed, his chest glistening with sweat.

"I need to collect a few things from the forest. Would you mind coming with me?"

He glances at where Tagiz is currently fighting with Rakiz, their swords clashing. I'm very carefully keeping my eyes away from him, his words still running through my mind.

He called the situation with Malis "complicated."

And he sure didn't deny he plans to mate with her.

I'm not an idiot. I can see neither of them have true feelings for each other. Malis seems to treat Tagiz as an older brother, and everyone knows she's in love with a warrior called Heric.

So why?

Hewex shifts, and I realize I'm staring into space.

"Sorry," I murmur. "Did you say something?"

"I asked if you'd prefer to go with Tagiz. He will be finished training soon."

"No," I say quickly. "I just need a few things, so there's no point waiting. If you're busy, I can grab someone else."

Hewex nods, his craggy face set in its usual scowl. I don't take it personally. Tagiz once told me Hewex prefers to be away from camp, hunting Voildi or checking traps. For whatever reason, Rakiz has decided to keep them both close right now.

"When are you going to teach me how to fight?" I ask as we walk out of the camp.

He glowers at me. "Ask Tagiz."

"You said you'd help me, Hewex." And I'm going to hold him to it.

He sighs. "Why do you want to learn how to fight? There are plenty of warriors here to protect you."

A feminist Hewex is not.

"I'm not saying I want to go into battle. I just want to be able to defend myself."

"Why don't you train with the other human females?"

My cheeks heat. "They're stronger and faster than me. I'm still recovering some of my stamina."

He sighs, and he's quiet as we move into the part of the forest where I'll find the plants I need.

"Meet me in the training arena at dawn," he says finally, and I almost do a little boogie.

Instead, I shoot him a grin. "Thank you."

My mind is wandering as we walk through the forest, and I collect some of the things I need along the way. Hewex trails behind me, and I take a deep breath, enjoying the feel of fresh air rushing through my lungs. It's funny, the things you take for granted until you learn they can be taken away at any moment.

One thing I learned as a nurse? Humans are resilient. The human body can tolerate indescribable trauma and survive—against almost insurmountable odds.

I don't know why some people make it and others don't. Even after so many years working to save lives, I still can't explain why some people fight through injuries and sickness that should have killed them and others succumb with little warning.

But I do know none of our days are guaranteed.

Not one.

I thought I understood this, when I was working with trauma patients on Earth. But it wasn't until I got up close and personal with my own death that I truly felt it down to my bones.

Now it's up to me to decide what to do with the rest of my life.

I spot some of the pink mushrooms I need at the base of a tree. I duck behind it and let out a shriek as white teeth flash and something nearly takes off my hand.

I can hear Hewex running toward me as I dart back, stumbling over a tree root sticking up from the ground and landing on my ass.

The tiny creature backs toward the tree, its fur raised as it hisses at me, and in spite of my shaking hands, my heart melts.

It's just a baby.

I get to my feet, lean around the tree, and give Hewex a smile.

"False alarm," I say as he approaches. "I...broke a nail."

He stares at me. I stare back at him.

Finally, he scowls and marches back across the small clearing to the tree he likes to lean against.

"Stay where I can see you," he orders.

"I'm just going to get some of those mushrooms." I point toward the tree, and the furred creature bares its teeth at me again. Hewex nods.

"Hey, baby," I murmur softly as I approach, and the creature hisses at me again. It's a light gray color, with pointed ears and huge, round eyes. Its fur sticks up in all directions, and while it has a mouth full of sharp teeth, my mouth twitches at its fuzzy coat.

My smile drops. All that fur can't hide the fact it looks half starved.

"You poor little thing," I whisper.

The creature eyes me, teeth still bared, but it's pressing its back into the tree, obviously terrified. I reach into my basket and pull out a hunk of bread and some fruit I grabbed for breakfast. I'm sure this tiny little beast would prefer meat, but I place the food on the ground anyway.

"Zoey." Hewex's voice is coming closer, and the creature hisses again.

"I'm coming." I turn to the little fluff ball, who seems to be eyeing both me and the food suspiciously. "I'll bring you back some meat if you're still here tomorrow," I croon to it before hurrying back to where Hewex is waiting.

Tagiz

"What are we going to do?" Malis is pacing in front of me, twisting her hands together. "Heric is getting tired of waiting for me, Tagiz. He loves me, but even he can only take so much. I keep telling him we're going to figure this out, but he's beginning to believe I don't truly want him." Her eyes fill with tears, and I sigh.

"Would you like me to speak with him?"

She shrugs. "I don't know. I doubt he'll listen to you."

I pinch the bridge of my nose in an attempt to fight off the headache that's brewing. Heric likely believes I am his enemy, the male who may take the female he loves from him. He may not understand I feel the same way about this mating as Malis does.

If it were Zoey in Malis's position, it would take all my strength not to kill the other warrior.

"What about *your* female, Tagiz? Do you believe she will wait forever? If the humans fix their ship, Zoey may decide she is tired of wishing for a warrior who treats her so casually."

My heart twists and my fists clench with the need to tie Zoey to me before she gives up and leaves me forever.

I take a deep breath, forcing myself to focus.

I know what Malis is doing. She is hoping I will be the one to end this mating. Braxian males are territorial and possessive, and she knows I am close to throwing Zoey over my shoulder and taking her away from this tribe. Forever.

If I am the one to act, Malis will have fewer consequences. Her parents will be upset, but they will not be able to blame her for my actions. And she will be free to mate with Heric.

I give her a look that tells her I know what she is thinking, and her cheeks turn red. She throws up her hands but continues pacing.

"We need a plan," I murmur.

"What if you spoke with Rakiz?" Malis asks.

I shrug. "Rakiz has more than enough to concern him,

especially now with the birth of his daughter. He will simply say forced matings are banned in his tribe."

While neither Malis nor I want to be mated, it is the thought of disappointing our parents that keeps us locked in this situation.

"I know you fear your father's reaction," Malis begins, and I shrug. Malis may believe she understands the loyalty I have to my father, but she has no idea just how much I owe him.

My kradi bells ring, and I turn, finding Hewex waiting.

"We have a meeting with Dexar," he says. "I passed your father in the food kradi, and he asked me to tell you to come to him when we are finished."

I glance at Malis. Her hands are shaking, and I blink as she suddenly lunges at me, her hands fisting in my shirt.

"Please, Tagiz. Please make it right. I can't take this anymore." She buries her face in my shirt and sobs. My eyes meet Hewex's, and his disapproval is clear on his face as he watches Malis lose control, wrapping her arms around me.

Hewex likes Zoey. He has told me multiple times if I do not want the little healer, there are plenty of other warriors who do.

I want to tell him this is not what it looks like, but I bite my tongue. If Hewex does not believe me honorable after all these years, then he never truly knew me.

CHAPTER SIX

Z oey

I'm at the training arena before the sun has fully risen, sweat from my nightmares still drying on my skin.

Hewex is waiting for me, his face set in its usual scowl.

"I know I agreed to train you," he says, and my heart sinks. "But Rakiz has ordered security to be increased around this camp and across his territory. I will be leaving for a few days to guard the northwest sector of our territory." I sigh, but he glances over his shoulder. "I've found someone else to train you instead."

I perk up at that, and Hewex nods to the other side of the arena, where a warrior is waiting. I've seen him around camp, but we've never actually met.

"This is Kroniz," Hewex says. "He has agreed to teach you some basic skills."

Kroniz nods at me, his eyes curious.

"I'm Zoey," I say. "I'm not expecting to be able to beat

anyone in an actual fight. I'd just like to be able to hold my own and maybe have a few tricks up my sleeve."

Kroniz nods. "From what I have learned about human females, you are vicious when cornered. I believe I will be able to teach you what you need to know."

My cheeks heat further, and his smile widens.

Hewex narrows his eyes at us. "Well. There's no harm in learning some hand-to-hand. Perhaps some basic knife skills," he grumbles.

"We've got this covered," Kroniz says, and Hewex glances at me, suddenly looking uncertain. Finally, he shrugs, stalking off without another word.

I've grown used to Hewex's curmudgeon ways by now, and Kroniz doesn't seem concerned either, gesturing for me to follow him to the far side of the training arena.

"Before we get started, I need to know what I'm working with." He reaches for me, and the movement is so sudden my hands automatically come up defensively.

Kroniz pauses, evaluating my stance. "Don't move."

He leans forward, adjusting my hands until they're no longer palm up, fingers curled and nails ready to claw. He folds my fingers and turns my hands until they're fisted.

Immediately, I feel like a badass.

"Fights are won and lost in moments," he murmurs. "Human females are small. You only have one chance to take an attacker by surprise. You must instinctively take this stance. From here, you can strike out, block, and evade a punch."

Kroniz makes me place my hands by my sides and walk across the training arena. As I walk, he jumps at me, getting into my personal space. The first few times, my hands instinctively come up the same way—palms up, fingers like claws. But by the time the sun has fully risen, my hands are fisted when they rise, and I'm ready for the next step.

"That's all for today," Kroniz says, and I blink, realizing the arena is beginning to fill with Braxians.

"Thank you," I say. "I really appreciate this. I don't expect to suddenly be a fighter. I don't even *want* to be a fighter. I'd just like to feel a little more confident."

He nods. "I owe Hewex a favor, and I'm happy to spend it teaching a pretty human female how to fight."

I blink at the teasing note in his voice. "Well, thank you," I say. "I better go. I need to collect a few herbs for Moni."

He narrows his eyes at me. "In the forest?"

I barely refrain from muttering about overprotective males. I was hoping to be able to feed the little furry animal alone, but obviously all the warriors in this camp have been given the same orders we've been given.

I sigh. "Would you like to come with me?"

He nods, a slow smile spreading across his face.

Not for the first time, I wish it were a warrior like Kroniz who made my heart thump harder. I sigh. Life would be so much more convenient if we could choose who we loved.

Kroniz leans on the wooden fence that encircles the training arena. Across the wide space, near the opposite fence, Tagiz has arrived for his morning training session, and he's currently chatting with a few of the younger warriors. They look up to him, constantly asking him to correct their form or spend a few hours sparring with them. He seems to have endless patience, only declining if he has a meeting.

He glances over his shoulder, his eyes unerringly finding mine. His face lights up in a way that makes me warm inside, but it quickly goes blank when his gaze shifts to the warrior next to me.

"Zoey?"

Kroniz is saying something, and I turn my attention back to him. His eyes are curious as he glances between me and Tagiz. "Is there something I should know about you and Tagiz?"

I shrug. "It's complicated."

He glances back at Tagiz, who is staring steadily at us. Cax—one of the younger warriors who hero-worships Tagiz—says something to get Tagiz's attention, and his gaze finally leaves us.

Kroniz shifts next to me. "I thought he was going to mate with Malis?"

I wince, and Kroniz grimaces at whatever he sees on my face. "I've hurt you. I'm sorry."

"No," I say. "You're right. He *is* going to mate with her. At least, he's meant to. I better get those herbs before Moni wonders where I am."

Kroniz turns away, finding his shirt from where he slung it over the side of the fence earlier. Tagiz's eyes find mine again, and I feel my chin jut out.

"Let's go."

Kroniz chats as we walk to the edge of the forest. He asks me about my life on Earth and seems impressed when I explain my duties in the hospital. He tells me about his family, and before I know it, I'm in the small clearing where I last saw the furry animal.

"If you want to wait here, I'll just be moseying around this area."

His eyes harden slightly at that, and I raise my hands threateningly, fisting them like he taught me.

He laughs. "Fine. Let me know if you need any help."

I nod and reach out, grabbing a few leaves off a bari plant. They're not good for anything except freshening your breath, and I chew on one as I make my way to the tree where I last saw the tiny, hissing creature.

My heart sinks as I stare at the empty spot.

This is a good thing, Zoey. It ate your food and went on its way.

I turn with a sigh, unsure why I'm so upset. Then I freeze as a deep growl sounds behind me.

I whirl, my heart racing, and I let out a strangled laugh as I survey the tiny animal. It's about the size of a Jack Russell, although I'd never get it confused with a dog. I've seen pictures of baby wolves, and its fluffy coat has some resemblance, but its claws glint in the sunlight as it bares its teeth at me.

"Did you make that scary sound?"

I keep my voice low and calm, slowly reaching into my pocket for the meat I brought with me.

It shuffles forward as I place the meat on the ground, and my chest tightens as I realize it's only walking on three legs.

I crane my neck, attempting to get a look at the animal's hind leg. It ignores me, digging into the meat as if it hasn't eaten for a while. And from the look of it, it probably hasn't.

"Poor little baby," I murmur.

I freeze as it finishes its meat and steps closer, nuzzling against my legs. I place my basket on the ground and crouch, careful not to let it get too close to my face. This is a wild animal on an alien planet. I may be softhearted, but I'm not an idiot.

The animal licks at my fingers, and my heart melts. "Okay," I murmur. "Turns out I *am* an idiot. You have two choices," I tell it, wishing it could actually understand me. "I can bring you back some food tomorrow, or you can hop in my basket today and I'll take you back to my kradi. I'll give you a bath, take a look at that leg, and give you as much food as you can eat."

The creature ignores me, and I laugh. "Wishful thinking, huh? I'll bring you back some more food tomorrow. Maybe if I describe you to Moni, she'll be able to tell me what you are."

I get to my feet. The little alien wolf doesn't seem to like that. It hisses at me, and I simply raise one eyebrow, hands on my hips.

It limps over to me, takes the hem of my dress in its mouth, and tugs.

"Zoey?"

"Just picking some berries. I'll be right there."

Something tells me if the warriors see the size of the teeth on this little dude or dudette, they're not going to be happy with me hanging around it.

The little beast turns its head, snarling in Kroniz's direction. I barely suppress a laugh, reaching down for my basket.

My mouth drops open as the creature jumps into the basket before curling up and gazing at me as if waiting to see what I'll do next.

"Okay, then. I'll take you back to camp and look at your leg, and then you're coming straight back to the wild, little fur monster."

I pick up the basket, grunting slightly at the heavier weight. Kroniz barely glances at me when I return, his eyes scanning the small clearing as if evaluating it for threats.

The fluff ball seems to know it should keep a low profile. It's curled up in my basket, head down on its paws, looking about as threatening as a kitten.

I snort as I place the basket down, leaning over to grab some retia leaves to steep in a tea for those with indigestion.

I shove the leaves in my pocket, dig for some hexo root, and haul the basket up onto my hip.

"I will carry your basket," Kroniz offers, pushing off the tree and striding toward me.

"Oh no, I'm fine, thanks."

He frowns but finally nods, and we begin to walk back to camp. I almost laugh as I glance down and realize the little fur ball is sleeping.

Kroniz seems distracted, his attention elsewhere, and he smiles at me as we get to the camp gates before calling a goodbye as he stalks back in the direction of the training arena. I shrug, hauling the basket back to my kradi.

I place it down, and the fur ball jumps out on three legs.

I doubt the little animal will let me look at its injured leg until I've built up some more trust. We watch each other silently, and then I sigh, crouching to examine it.

"So. You're a boy, huh?" He ignores that, and I hold out my hand for him to sniff. "I need to go get you some more food. It's probably best if you stay here for now."

He ignores that too, lying down on the floor and curling into a ball. I should probably tie him up, but I can't bring myself to. Once you've looked out at the world from inside a cage, you think twice about taking anyone else's freedom.

"I'll be right back," I promise.

***

Tagiz

I almost slam into Zoey as she exits her kradi, and my hands automatically steady her as she jolts back in surprise.

"Tagiz..."

She glances over her shoulder at her kradi, and fury begins to climb up my spine.

"Why do you look guilty, little healer?"

"Huh? I don't know what you're talking about."

"Is Kroniz in your kradi?"

"What? Don't be ridiculous." She scowls at me, and I can see the truth on her face. Zoey is a terrible liar. Every time she attempted to tell me her ribs "didn't hurt that bad" or she "didn't need Moni's sleeping tonic," her eyes would dart away, as if it was impossible for her to look at me while telling an untruth.

That doesn't change the fact she's still practically vibrating with guilt. And she's now blocking my way into her kradi, her hands on her hips as she glares at me.

Whatever it is she's hiding, it's in her kradi.

"I can't even believe you would ask that," she says, and I focus on her face. "You think I'm rolling around with someone else?"

I shake my head. "No, little healer. I'm sorry."

She searches my face. I don't want to admit my jealousy has gotten the best of me. Kroniz is an honorable male and well liked by almost everyone in this tribe. Most importantly, he is not expected to mate with anyone.

The male can choose his fate.

So can you, a little voice whispers. *Is your father's happiness worth losing your female?*

I blink, realizing Zoey is staring up at me.

"Tagiz?"

For the first time, I realize why I am hesitant to disappoint my father.

Because he may not just be disappointed.

He may disown me.

"Tagiz?"

I blink again, drinking in the sight of Zoey's beautiful face. The sun is high in the sky, highlighting the tiny freckles scattered across her nose as she scrunches it in confusion.

I want to watch her give me that same look whenever she is exasperated with me for the rest of my life.

I want to—

Something growls. Zoey glances over her shoulder and then stares at the ground.

"What was that?"

"My stomach," she lies. "I'm hungry. Will you walk with me to the food kradi?"

Her stomach does let out a rumble at that, and she casts me a triumphant look from beneath her lashes. But I'm not fooled.

My little healer is hiding something in her kradi.

"Zoey—"

"Hurry up, Tagiz. I have things to do today."

I will be patient. But I will learn what is in that kradi before nightfall.

Zoey links her arm through mine and chats to me about the forest, the weather, and the new human females. I make noises in the right places, but I'm distracted—both by whatever it is Zoey is hiding and by thoughts of my relationship with my father.

Zoey falls silent, and I watch her, realizing her mind is also elsewhere.

I take her to the food kradi, pretending not to notice her take an extra serving of meat. She doesn't eat either the extra meat or the meat on her plate. Instead, she folds it up in a large cloth and puts it in her pocket when she thinks I'm not looking.

My spine straightens at the thought of whatever made

that growl. Zoey has a large heart. A soft heart that radiates love and kindness. But there are animals on this planet that could kill her in an instant.

"Who did you take with you to the forest today, little healer?"

She takes a bite of her bread and angles her head, her gaze on my face as she swallows.

"Kroniz."

If he has allowed my female to bring an animal back from the forest that could hurt her, I will kill him. The thought fills me with satisfaction, and I scowl. It's my jealousy that makes me wish him gone.

I walk Zoey back to her kradi. She smiles brightly at me, and I turn as if to leave. Her sigh of relief is audible, and I shake my head, amused despite myself. Zoey does not have a deceptive bone in her body.

She walks into her kradi, and I follow her in, ignoring her gasp of outrage as I push her behind me.

"A karja?" I turn to stone. The beast may be a baby, but karja grow incredibly fast.

I glower at Zoey, and she tilts her head as she gazes at the sleeping karja. It opens its eyes to slits and shows me its teeth.

Zoey elbows me in the ribs. "Move out of the way, you big, dumb warrior!"

My mouth twitches at that, but I stay standing between Zoey and the karja.

"It's dangerous, Zoey."

"He's a baby! Look at his little leg. He couldn't survive in the wild. He's starving."

I sigh as I take in the poor creature. It is indeed thin, but I know too well it is the beast with nothing to lose that is the most dangerous.

"Give me the meat."

Zoey hands it to me wordlessly, but I can feel her annoyance. I crouch, holding out the food, and the karja shows me its teeth again but creeps forward.

It snatches a hunk of meat from my hand before backing away to chew it. But it returns, eventually eating calmly from my hand, and I glance up at Zoey.

"So?" she asks.

"This was a dangerous thing to do, little healer, but I understand you have a soft heart. If you want to treat the karja's leg, I will help you."

She gazes at me for a long moment but finally nods. The karja sniffs at my hand, looking for more food, and then backs away, lying back down with a huff.

Zoey's smile is blinding. "Okay. Wait right here. I'll get some more food to distract it and stop by the healers' kradi to get what I need."

She doesn't take long, and I spend the time watching the karja, who ignores me. It gets to its feet with a growl as Zoey approaches the kradi but immediately lies back down when Zoey steps back inside.

"Okay." Zoey smiles at me. "Let's do this."

I slowly feed the karja meat, making it last while Zoey examines its back leg.

"Poor thing," she murmurs. "It's broken. We need to set it so I can splint it, and it's going to be painful. I don't want to give him any of the painkillers we use in the healers' kradi in case he reacts badly to them." She glances at me, and I nod.

"Tell me when."

She takes the karja's leg between her hands and counts down. I wrap my hand around the karja's muzzle, and the creature lets out a sound that brings tears to Zoey's eyes as she sets its leg. The karja attempts to snap at me when I release its muzzle but takes the last of the meat as Zoey splints its leg.

"There, all done now," Zoey croons to the karja. "You were such a good boy."

"What will we do now?"

"We need to wait for his leg to heal before we release him back into the wild. Maybe we could set up a small, fenced area for him near the forest."

The karja sniffs at my empty hand and moves away when it realizes I'm out of food. I tense as it walks toward Zoey, but the creature curls up in her lap, closing his eyes as she gently strokes its fluffy ears.

I sigh. Somehow, I am unsurprised my little healer has tamed a karja.

"We will talk about this."

Zoey scowls at me but glances back at the sleeping karja and obviously decides she doesn't want to disturb it because she gently places it on a fur, takes my arm, and leads me out of her kradi.

"Now it's your turn to eat," I say, and she rolls her eyes.

"Were you not just with me when I ate lunch? Did I imagine that?"

"You didn't eat any meat, little healer."

She scowls at me. "Why am I not surprised you noticed that? I'm honestly not hungry anymore, Tagiz. But I could use a walk, and then I might see if Moni needs help."

She links her arm through mine, and I smile down at her.

"If you're sure you're not hungry, I have something to show you," I say. I lead her through the camp and behind Rakiz's tashiv. Our camp is close to the river, and Ivy and Vrex had their mating ceremony in the small clearing close by. But behind that clearing, through the trees, a small stream flows into the river, and it's quiet. Peaceful.

"Wow," she says when we arrive. "This is gorgeous."

I pull her even closer, inhaling her scent. "I used to come here when I was a boy. Our tribe moved much more often then, but whenever we camped in this area, I would sit on one of those flat rocks and watch the water for hours. Just thinking."

Zoey smiles up at me, and I give in to my urges, cupping her cheek and covering her mouth with mine. She sighs against me, her body softening, and it takes all my self-control to pull back. "You are so very sweet, little healer," I murmur, brushing her hair behind her ear.

Her cheeks pinken, and I grin as she clears her throat, turning back to the water. Zoey is determined to pretend she is unaffected by me.

"What did you think about?" she asks.

"The usual things young males think about. Becoming a fierce warrior. Bedding females. Protecting the king."

She bursts out laughing as I knew she would, and the sound draws a smile to my own lips. She said she wanted to check in with Moni, so I guide her back around Rakiz's tashiv, taking her the long way toward the healers' kradi, toward my own kradi.

"Where are we going?"

"I have something for you, little healer."

Her eyes widen, and her hand clutches at my arm. "What kind of something?"

I study her face. My Zoey enjoys surprises. While she was recovering, I would bring her fruit, sweet cakes, and small trinkets, hiding them behind my back as she attempted to guess what I might be concealing from her. No matter how tired she was that day, her eyes would light up.

That time was simpler for us. My father had not yet begun to be threatened by Zoey, had not yet started his incessant nagging that I mate with Malis. I had...time to spend with my little healer.

"Tagiz?"

I shake myself back to the present. "You will need to be patient," I tell her, enjoying her playful pout. I have carved something for her that will make her life easier when she collects her strange herbs and flowers.

I lead her toward my kradi, freezing as Heric stalks toward us, his expression enraged.

CHAPTER SEVEN

Tagiz

I thrust Zoey behind me as Heric approaches. He is usually a mild-mannered male, but from the look of frustrated rage in his eyes, he has been pushed too far.

"You believe you can mate with my female?" he growls, slamming his palms against my chest.

Zoey gasps behind me, and I grind my teeth, attempting to ignore the curious eyes that begin to turn our way.

"Be careful, Heric," I murmur.

He laughs bitterly. "Or you will challenge me to meet you in the training arena? You believe that would be worse than stealing my mate from me?"

Zoey makes a tiny sound in the back of her throat and attempts to move past me. I snag her wrist, holding her close, and she growls a curse under her breath.

"You know I don't want to mate with Malis," I say, reaching for patience.

He snorts, his gaze moving to Zoey. His eyes lighten, and he strikes me where he knows he will do the most damage.

"Then why has your father announced you and Malis will be mated by the next full moon?"

I feel Zoey flinch. She reacts as if she has been hit, and I immediately shift my gaze from Heric, who growls, affronted.

"It's not true," I tell her. She refuses to look at me, and I grind my teeth in frustration, suddenly wanting nothing more than to slam my fist into Heric's face.

He scoffs. "Your father wouldn't lie."

My jaw protests as my teeth clamp together even harder. Of course my father would lie. He would do whatever he felt necessary to force my hand.

I open my mouth, but Zoey takes advantage of my moment of inattention and deftly slips her wrist out of my hand. Who taught her that move? She's gone before I can snatch her back to me, and Heric lets out a low laugh at whatever he sees on my face.

I move to follow Zoey, and Heric steps in front of me. I wrestle with my temper, but I'm close to the edge. "We have never had a problem before," I bite out. "Even with everything Malis's and my parents have planned. But if you ever get between me and that female again, I will *end* you."

I shove past him, dodging curious tribe members as I hurry after Zoey. She's almost running, obviously desperate to get away from me, and it makes something wild inside me sit up and take notice.

I will follow her until the end of time.

"Zoey."

She glances over her shoulder at me, her eyes narrowing as she sees me following her. "What do you want?"

"You."

Her eyes widen slightly, but a bitter laugh leaves her. "No, you don't. Not really."

Not want her? I stare at her, stunned, and she snorts, turning to walk away.

I stalk her, following close as she makes her way back to her kradi. We're near my kradi now though, and I'm not letting her run away from me this time.

Zoey picks up her pace, attempting to ignore me, but I can tell by the way she rubs at the back of her neck that she knows I'm still behind her.

I pull her to a stop outside my kradi, and her nose scrunches as she scowls at me.

"Why are you following me, Tagiz?"

She's still furious, and her blazing blue eyes, flushed face, and fisted hands make my gut clench.

I stop fighting it.

I bury my hand in her hair, pulling her close as I take her mouth. She tastes like sunshine, and her gasp of surprise is music to my soul. She immediately softens against me, her body well aware of what her mind refuses to believe.

She. Is. Mine.

I lift her into my arms, and she squeaks against me. I keep my mouth pressed to hers as I walk into my kradi and lower her onto the furs.

It's difficult, but I manage to pull away long enough to find the buttons of her dress.

"Shouldn't you be planning your mating with Malis?" she growls.

"Stubborn," I chuckle, and she tenses. For a moment, I think she might push me away, and I lean down, pressing my lips to the soft skin of her neck as I breathe her in.

I shudder, and her hands come up, sliding into my hair as she holds me to her.

I want to rip her dress from her and mark every inch of her with my body. I want to ravage her, plunder her, teach her she will always be mine.

But I gentle my touch, breaking away for long enough to help her out of her dress.

Zoey was made to be savored.

She's wide-eyed as she glances up at me, confusion and helpless lust written all over her face.

She's naked in moments, and I can't help but stare. She blushes, and even her chest turns pink.

"Tagiz," she murmurs, attempting to cover her breasts from my avid gaze.

I catch her hands. "You're so beautiful." I'm breaking all the rules for her. I know this will make it worse for both of us, but I can't walk away.

We deserve this.

I lick and nip across her breasts until her hands are once again pulling me close. I love that. I love how she urges me on, demanding more from me.

I'll give her everything I have, and it still won't be enough.

I grind against her as I take her nipple in my mouth, and she gasps, her hands moving to my back as she opens her legs for me.

I kiss my way down her stomach, desperate for the taste of her.

"Later," she gasps, urging me back up. "I need you inside me. Now."

I frown at her, but she juts out her chin again, and it's so adorable I laugh.

"Later, I'm going to lick you until you scream," I promise her.

I want to make her blush like this for the rest of my life.

But it will be some other male who gets to hear her soft giggles and languid sighs. My eye twitches at the thought, and she frowns up at me.

"What's wrong?"

I press against her, and she urges me on. She's hot and wet, and I freeze.

"What are you doing?" she asks.

She lifts her hips, and I curse, my hands falling to her, holding her still.

"Attempting not to embarrass myself, little healer."

She sends me a wicked smile. "Go ahead."

I shake my head and reach for control. Then I sink into her, studying her face as her eyes flutter shut.

I've imagined this moment a thousand times. But my imagination couldn't come close to the feel of her beneath me, her breasts against my chest, her head tipping back as a moan leaves her throat.

I pull back and then thrust again, and she writhes under me, arching her back as she moans. I give her what she needs, twisting my hips as I grind against her. She wraps her legs around my waist, and I fight not to come.

I pause again, and she gives me a saucy wink. The minx is trying to make me lose control.

I pick up the pace, my hand coming up to play with her breast. It's soft and firm, her nipple hard against my palm. I stroke over it and then do it again as she goes wetter around me.

"Hmm," I murmur, leaning down to take her nipple in my mouth. Thanks to the size difference between us, I have to stop thrusting as I do, which is a good thing because she lets out a low groan that almost makes me lose control.

"Tagiz," she sighs, and I plunge back into her. Her nails dig into my arms, creating marks I wish would become permanent. Then everyone would know she is mine. That she claims *me* back.

I never want to leave these furs.

She quivers beneath me, her breath catching, and I thrust deeper. I hit a spot that makes her yelp, but it seems to be a good yelp because she clenches around me. So I do it again. And again.

"Oh my God, Tagiz," she moans, and I grind against her small bud with every thrust until she's gasping, her head twisting from side to side as she tightens her legs around my waist.

My balls tighten, and my shaft swells, the pressure warning me just in time. I move my thumb to her sex, almost losing it at the feel of her wide open for me. I stroke against her pearl, and she lets out a dry sob.

She clamps down around me like a fist, her breath catching, and I see stars as we come together, clutching each other close.

She pants, her eyes sliding closed, and I can't help it. I press kisses against every inch of her face.

She smiles, her eyes still closed, and I pull away, hauling her into my arms.

That was both the best and the worst thing I could have done.

Zoey

My stomach rumbles as I wake up, Tagiz still wrapped around me. I must have slept through the afternoon.

I shift and glance up. Tagiz is awake, obviously deep in thought as he examines the roof of his kradi, his brow creased.

"Hey," I say, and my voice is slightly hoarse.

He smiles down at me, then lifts me until I'm in the air, hovering over him. His strength is insane. He pulls me down until we can kiss, and I sink into him.

"What are you thinking, little healer?"

I chew on my lip. "I'm thinking about your dad. What's with this mating with Malis, and why does he think he can run your life?"

Tagiz closes his eyes. "Calix...it's more complicated than you think."

"I'm relatively intelligent," I point out. "Explain it to me."

He sighs. "My father's family has long been focused on bloodlines. It is the strongest and the bravest who are trusted to fight beside the tribe king, and it is an honor to be in his inner circle. He was one of the king's guards, as was his father before him and his father, for centuries."

I nod. "And now you are too."

"Yes. But...my father is not my...true sire."

My mouth drops open at that. For all his obsession with bloodlines, Calix isn't even Tagiz's real father?

"How did that happen?"

"My tribe was small but fierce. Our qatai was obsessed with growing our territory, and his advisors had convinced him he would be able to take this tribe."

"I'm guessing that didn't go so well."

He shakes his head, leaning down to press a kiss against my forehead, and I snuggle closer to him.

"No. My father died on the first day of fighting, leaving me alone. My mother had died of a sickness three revolutions earlier."

My chest aches for the child Tagiz must have been. Left all alone in what was guaranteed to be a bloodbath.

He clears his throat. "The qatai put a sword in my hand and ordered me to take my father's place."

"How old were you?"

"I had seen seven summers."

I lift my head in shock. "You were just a kid. Why would he do that?"

Tagiz shrugs. "My father was gone, dead in battle, and it was becoming evident we had no real chance against this tribe. If we successfully retreated, I would be another mouth that he would be responsible for feeding. I assume he wanted his enemies to take care of the problem."

Rage makes my hands shake, and I fist them, imagining a tiny Tagiz clutching his sword, his eyes wide and terrified with the knowledge he was about to die.

"That son of a bitch."

Tagiz laughs, lifting my fist and opening my hand so he can press a kiss to my palm.

"I could barely lift the sword he gave me when he sent me to the front lines. Calix appeared out of nowhere, and I attacked him. I knew I was going to die, but my father would have wanted me to die an honorable death with a sword in my hand."

My heart pounds like a drum. "What happened?"

He laughs. "Calix knocked my sword away, cuffed me around the head, and pushed me toward one of his men. They put me in the qatai's tashiv. I could hear the sounds of the battle, the noise of swords clanging, of warriors dying. But my clearest memory is the taste of the meat the servants fed me. I hadn't eaten for three days."

I glance at his face, and he gives me a half smile, but his eyes are wounded. His tribe threw him away. His father died for his tribe king, and the bastard wouldn't even protect a seven-year-old kid.

Tagiz sighs, stroking my hair. "Rakiz had been allowed to watch some of the battle. When he returned to find me in his father's tashiv, he glowered at me and told me his father was going to string me up as an example to any other tribes that thought to attack."

"Uh-oh."

He laughs. "I believed him. So I decided if I was going to die, I was going to take the future tribe king down with me."

I smile. "Of course you did."

"Calix arrived to find us tangled and rolling around on the floor, each with a knife at the other's throat. He pulled us both up by our shirts and gave us a tongue lashing I can still remember to this day. Then he offered me a choice. He would provide me with three days of rations and a sword and would allow me to leave the tribe. Or I could stay and be raised as his son."

"I'm confused by this. You've said he was obsessed with…"

"Bloodlines? Yes. But he and his mate had been attempting to have a child of their own for four revolutions. His mate had been chosen by his father due to the exceptional warriors in her line, and my father was beginning to realize she was barren."

My teeth are clenched as I sit up. Sure, Calix may have saved Tagiz from certain death, but the more I learn about him, the less I like. Besides, I'd bet the last hair band I have hidden beneath my furs that Calix wouldn't have adopted Tagiz if he'd had kids of his own.

"You know, it's not just women who are responsible for getting pregnant. Your father might be sterile."

He frowns at that. "Sterile," he says in English, and I realize there's no translation in Braxian.

Typical.

I explain the concept, giggling at the incredulous expression on his face.

"Are you sure?"

I angle my head and give him a look. "I'm sure."

"Hmm." He thinks about this for a long moment. "My father is unaware of this."

"I'm happy to explain the concept to him," I say sweetly, and he laughs, wrapping his arm around me and pulling me back down to him.

"So," I say. "Calix offered you a choice."

"Yes. He said he had been impressed with the bravery I showed when I attempted to attack him. He knew males older than me who were unable to lift the sword I had swung at him. He explained his family had a long tradition of serving the king. If he raised me as his son, I would be expected to train harder than I had ever imagined and protect the future tribe king with my life."

I smile at the thought of Rakiz and Tagiz sneering at each other as Calix made that proclamation.

"I bet you liked the sound of that."

He laughs. "I wasn't going to turn down the best offer I'd ever heard. An offer that included joining one of the biggest and most powerful Braxian tribes on Agron. Rakiz protested, but Calix told him he would be happy to inform his father about how Rakiz had attempted to kill one of his 'prisoners' before he could be interrogated."

"So you were raised as Calix's son."

He nods, and I stroke my finger over one of his pecs as I consider everything he's told me.

Tagiz may think he owes Calix everything, but I see the guy for who he is. A master manipulator who only cares about himself and who *he* believes Tagiz should be.

He took a scared orphan and raised him to believe he only had one option in life. He raised him with the belief he was in debt to Calix because he saved him from being slaughtered on the battlefield.

"Can I ask you something?"

"Of course."

"Do you think any of the other warriors in this camp would have killed you that day?"

He's silent for a long moment. "No. Honor is everything in this tribe, and there is no honor in killing a child."

"But you didn't know that at the time."

"No. In my tribe, we fought for everything."

"So you automatically felt beholden to Calix for saving your life."

He tenses. "He did save my life. He didn't need to take me as his own, Zoey."

"I know. But do you think Rakiz's dad truly would've let you leave his tribe with nothing but some food and a sword?"

"No. But I didn't know that then."

"Exactly."

"What are you saying?"

I choose my words carefully. As much as I'm beginning to loathe Calix, he's still Tagiz's father.

"I'm saying maybe you feel like you need to live up to the idea of what Calix wants you to be simply because you feel like you owe him for taking you in as a child. But any decent person would've done the exact same thing."

He considers this. "You raise good points, but it changes nothing. I am my father's only son. The son he chose. Without him and my mother, I would have been another camp orphan, perhaps given to parents who would not have overseen my training. Parents who would not have ensured I would be a strong warrior."

I nod as I pretend to let it go. But I'm not letting anything go. I don't doubt Calix loves his son. How could he not? But by offering that scared, lonely seven-year-old a choice in exchange for being raised by him, he made it clear the home he offered came with strings. Do as Calix said, live the life he wanted him to lead, and Tagiz would have a home.

Tagiz kisses my forehead. Then my cheek. Then he gently brushes my lips with his before working his way down my neck, making me squirm in need as his warm breath tickles the shell of my ear.

I shiver against him, and he lets out a low laugh as I arch, my hands reaching for him in an attempt to drag him closer.

He takes both my wrists in one hand, holding them between us.

"My turn," he murmurs. He leans down, and his lips are hungry, demanding more as his tongue conquers my mouth. I attempt to lift my hands again, ridiculously turned on as he squeezes my wrists gently, making it clear he's the one in charge.

His eyes are dark as he slowly pulls away, and I lick my lips. He lets out a rough curse before immediately taking my mouth again.

Suddenly, he's pushing back the furs, his gaze once again drinking in my naked body.

My cheeks burn, and he continues kissing his way down, stopping to nuzzle at my breasts, his tongue flicking each nipple until they're both hard and aching, desperate for more.

"Tagiz," I groan, and he licks at my lower belly, right above my pubic bone, then blows cool air over my skin.

My thighs clench.

His hand finally releases my wrists, and I fist the furs beneath me as he moves his attention further south.

His hand cups me like he owns me, a low growl leaving his throat as his fingers slide through my wetness, making me beg.

"Tagiz, please."

"You rushed me last night, little healer. I was like an untried warrior as I got lost in the wonders of your body. Now I get to explore you properly."

I groan as he pinches my clit. "Explore me later."

He laughs. And then he's settling between my thighs, inhaling the scent of me as my cheeks burn. He pushes my thighs further apart, and his tongue plunges into me, making me cry out at the sudden pleasure.

I rock into him, and his hands come up, holding my hips. He makes it clear he's in control and I'm just along for the ride.

And God, it's sexy.

His tongue rolls in firm circles along my clit, and my eyes slide shut as he pushes one large finger inside me.

"Open your eyes," he murmurs against me. "See who makes you feel like this, little healer."

I crack open my eyes, and he rewards me with more licking, more sucking, as another finger joins the first, and he angles them until he's flicking my G-spot.

My breath catches in my throat, and I let out long moan

as he uses the edge of his teeth on my clit, plunging his fingers into me at the same time.

I choke on my gasp.

He spreads my thighs even wider as he moves up my body, his jaw tight. I can feel him, hard and throbbing against my stomach, and I'm instantly desperate for him to be inside me again.

He moves up one of my legs until it's almost over his shoulder, and I cry out as he slides straight into me, not stopping until his balls are pressed up against me. He feels so big, filling me up until I don't know where I end and he begins.

He doesn't hesitate, instantly rocking into me, his pubic bone hitting my clit with each thrust. He's almost too big in this position, my hips angled up to allow him to hit spots inside me that haven't been hit before. But I'm so turned on, and his fingers pinch my nipple as he grinds into my clit. I begin to shake.

"Oh God..."

He laughs again, but it's clear from his tight jaw that he's barely holding on to his control.

I want to see him lose it.

I meet his thrusts, and he grinds down harder, almost in retaliation. He fists my hair, and the slight pain is enough to throw me over the edge as he rams into my G-spot, slamming into my clit at the same time.

I come so hard I see stars, and I can't even talk as he continues to thrust, immediately sending me back into nirvana.

He lets out a long, low growl, stilling as he empties himself into me. He buries his head in my neck, and I bring up my hands, clutching at him, reveling in the weight of his body on top of mine. He's careful not to crush me, and after a long moment, he rolls over until I'm sprawled on top of his chest.

"Wow" is all I can say.

His hand cups my butt possessively, and we lie silently, dozing for a while. Then he groans.

"I must go," he murmurs. "I have a meeting with Rakiz at sundown."

With a sigh, I watch him pull on his pants.

I feel more rested than I have in weeks, and I realize for the first time in longer than I can remember that I didn't dream.

I'm still exhausted, but obviously the key to a good nap is being wrapped in Tagiz's arms.

I snort at that, and Tagiz glances at me. I feel suddenly awkward.

"What are we, Tagiz?"

He reaches for his shirt, and as he pulls it on, my gaze gets stuck on his chest. I drag my attention up to his face, noting the hesitant way he glances at me.

Nothing has changed, I realize. Even after seeing how we are together, he's still going to go along with his father's plans and spend the rest of his life with a woman he considers just a friend.

"Can we discuss this later? I'm sorry, Zoey, but I must go."

I nod, my mind racing as he leans over and presses a kiss to my forehead.

I've been an idiot. But enough is enough. I have plenty to focus on here, amongst the Dokhalls, the ship, and the new human women. If Tagiz doesn't consider what we have to be worth pissing off his dad, then there's nothing I can do or say to make him think differently.

CHAPTER EIGHT

Z oey

I survey the karja as he finishes eating the last of his breakfast.

I'm getting a little worried he's going to end up too domesticated. According to Rakiz, karja are occasionally tamed by Braxian warriors. Once they choose to take food from their hands, they're loyal to them for the rest of their days.

"I'm sorry I took you from your home," I murmur to the fur ball as he sniffs at my shoes.

"Today you're going back to the wild. Where you belong."

The little karja ignores me, obviously unimpressed. He seems to know something is up though. Usually, he prances in place when I show him the makeshift leash Tagiz made for him. Today, he turns and buries his head beneath the soft furs of his bed.

Like everyone on this planet, the karja healed remarkably fast. He's also growing at an incredible rate. No longer is he the size of a Jack Russell. Instead, he reminds me of my neighbor's border collie.

"If you don't get back to your real home soon, you're going to forget all about it."

I pull the furs off him and attach the leash to his collar. I hated to put it on him, but even I could see the necessity of it, considering how many kids live in this camp.

"Okay, buddy." I try to keep my voice perky and excited, but my heart aches. I'll miss my slobbery alarm.

I walk the karja out of my kradi and toward the forest where I found him. Tagiz offered to meet me to help me say goodbye, and even though we're in a weird place right now, I took him up on that offer.

It's been eight days since I fell asleep in his arms. Tagiz has been away hunting for six of them, and we haven't had a chance to talk.

As far as I'm aware, nothing has changed. Tagiz still feels it's his duty to mate with who his father has chosen for him. And whenever I think about it, fury burns in my belly. Fury at both Tagiz's father for making his son feel so indebted to him and at Tagiz for not being willing to tell his father to fuck off.

I'm trying to give him space and time, but truthfully, I'm sick of the long nights staring at the roof of my kradi. I'm tired of wondering if Tagiz will ever choose me. And I'm scared the things I feel for him will soon be replaced with resentment.

My mother would expect more from me. She raised me to know my worth, to not end up living a life similar to hers. I believe, deep in my heart, Tagiz could be the one for me. But that doesn't mean I'll wait forever.

He angles his head when we approach, as if surprised to see us. It's not long after sunrise, and the camp is beginning to wake. I wanted to do this early, though, so I could say goodbye to the little fur ball in private.

Tagiz leans against the camp wall, looking relaxed. But I can see the tension in his shoulders and in the lines around his eyes.

"Zoey?"

I jolt, realizing I'm staring at Tagiz with a frown on my face. The karja makes a show of baring his teeth at Tagiz with a growl, then gives a full-body shake and pulls me forward until he can sniff at Tagiz's boots.

Tagiz leans down and runs his hand over the fur ball's fluffy ears.

No, Zoey. Stop thinking about how those hands felt on your body.

"Okay," I mutter. "Let's get this over with."

Tagiz nods, his eyes sympathetic. He falls into step with me, and we're both silent as we head toward the spot where I found the karja.

"Have you spent much time in the Seinex Forest?" I ask, and Tagiz glances at me.

"Yes. I was posted there with Hewex. We hunted Voildi and dismantled their traps."

"What's it like?"

Moni speaks of the Seinex Forest with something like reverence. There are things that grow there that are unable to be found anywhere else.

"It is...interesting. You won't remember, but we rode through the forest when we brought you back to camp." His mouth twists at the memory. "The trees look different from these ones." He nods to the forest that stretches out in front of us. "They're bone white, with few leaves. Things happen in that forest that cannot be explained. It's a dangerous place." He glances at my face and smiles. "And you want to go."

I nod vigorously. "Moni mentioned a few things we need to restock, and...I just want to check it out. For my own experiments."

"I'll take you."

I chew on my lip at that. If anything, I should be trying to spend less time with Tagiz, since my traitorous heart can't be trusted not to start fluttering in my chest every time he looks at me.

He seems to be waiting for an answer, so I nod, and he frowns at my response, opening his mouth.

The karja growls.

I glance down at him and realize he's growling at the forest, pulling on the leash. I kneel down and untie the leash from his collar.

"Whoa—"

Tagiz steps forward, catching me as the karja shoves past me, and I almost fall. The fur ball bolts into the forest, and I pout after him.

"You're welcome."

The corners of Tagiz's eyes are crinkled as he helps me back up to my feet. But we both turn toward the forest at the sounds of more growling.

Oh my God. What if the karja is trying to fight with a bigger, tougher animal?

I sprint after him, ignoring the branches that claw at my face and hair as I run toward the growling. Tagiz curses roughly behind me, following me, and I stop dead as I find the karja growling at a...tree.

"You ever hear about the karja that cried wolf?" I murmur. The karja tilts its head, growling even louder, and

Tagiz steps around me.

"Tracks," he says, inspecting the tree.

That's when I see it. Someone has brushed past this tree, scraping against the bark. Next to it, on the ground, a rock has been flipped over, the dent still evident in the ground, the rock's damp side pointing toward the sky.

The karja growls some more. He snaps his teeth at the tree, then looks up at me. I blink at him. He's even smarter than I thought.

"It's like he's trying to tell us something."

"Karja are intelligent," Tagiz says as he crouches near the tree, examining some dirt that has been kicked up.

"What do you think?" I ask, and he frowns, his eyes intent on the tracks.

"Something was here. Something that doesn't smell like Braxians or humans, if the karja's reaction is any indication."

I glance back toward camp. "They were watching us."

He nods. "It's likely the Dokhalls."

I kneel and scratch the karja behind the ears. "You're so smart," I coo. I lean down and unfasten the leather strap we've been using as a collar, and my heart breaks just a little.

"It's time for you to go and rejoin the world, little guy."

He places one paw on my knee, snuggling close. I run my finger over his nose, ignoring the way my eyes turn blurry as I get to my feet.

Tagiz is waiting, and he immediately wraps his arm around my shoulders. "You likely saved his life," he murmurs. "You have a large heart, little healer."

I attempt a smile, ignoring the tear that slides down my cheek. "Let's get this over with."

I refuse to look back as we make our way toward camp. The karja is a wild animal. I took him out of the wild to save his life, but he still belongs in the forest, where he can roam and hunt.

We get about halfway back to the camp before Tagiz sighs. He's been letting me pretend I'm not crying as I subtly wipe tears off my face, but he stops walking suddenly, turning back toward the forest.

"What are you—oh."

The karja is following us.

"You can't come back with us," I say. "You belong in the wild."

He ignores that, trotting closer.

Tagiz sighs again. "We will continue walking. He may grow bored as something in the forest draws his attention."

But he doesn't grow bored. And eventually, I'm standing at the camp gate, staring down at the karja as it blinks innocently up at me. Tagiz runs his hand over his mouth, and I glower at him.

"This is not funny," I hiss.

He gives in to his grin. "I am not surprised you have tamed yet another male, little healer. I'm only surprised you didn't see this coming."

I sigh. "What are we going to do?"

"Karja are usually tamed by patient warriors over many months or years. But this one has clearly decided you are its pack leader."

I sigh again, surveying the furry creature, who's giving me a "what are we hanging around here for" look. "I'm not really the leader type," I advise him.

He gives me a growl, then stalks past me, heading back into camp.

Tagiz's lips twitch, and I glare at him. He attempts to suppress his smile, finally throwing back his head in laughter.

I did not need to see how beautiful you look when you laugh. No, I did not need to see that at all, thank you very much.

I ignore the way my hands ache with the need to reach for him, but he doesn't seem to have the same concerns. He drags me close and takes my mouth, his tongue pushing past my lips...and all of my defenses.

I'm almost panting when he pulls away.

"I have had a bad morning," he murmurs. "Just a few moments with you and my day has turned around. This is the effect you have on everyone who knows you, little healer. Even your little karja is not immune."

I give in, allowing my body to relax against his as I breathe in the male scent of him. We're standing at the camp gates, where anyone could see us—including his father—but right now, I can't bring myself to care.

"Well," I finally say. "I guess I better give him a name."

***

Zoey

I'm eating lunch in one of my favorite places outside, close to Nevada's tashiv, when I spot Beth walking across the small clearing. I wave at her, and she changes course, plunking down next to me and helping herself to some of my fruit.

"What are you still doing here?" I ask. "Not that it isn't great to hang out, of course."

She smiles. "We're staying until we've solved this little Dokhall problem. Zarix and Dexar like the idea of consolidating our defenses with Rakiz."

I nibble on my lower lip, suddenly depressed. "Alexis must hate that. She's constantly ripped away from her tribe. And you have your dance classes..."

"It's okay. It's just a short-term thing. But you're right. This has gone on for long enough. We need some kind of plan to remove this threat once and for all."

We sit in companionable silence for a few minutes, both of us munching as we watch tribe members going about their days.

"How are you, Zoey?" Beth breaks the silence. "You seem...sad."

Not only is Beth ethereally beautiful and naturally graceful—even with the slight limp—but she's also one of the kindest women I know.

"I'm okay." I smile at her, but her brow creases, telling me she sees through my bullshit.

"Something happened."

I clear my throat, and the words come out before I'm aware I'm speaking them. "I slept with Tagiz. Multiple times."

Her eyes widen, and then she grins, but the smile disappears as she examines my face.

"You don't seem all that pleased by this new development," she murmurs.

I laugh, but my throat feels clogged up, and the sound is closer to a sob.

"Hey." She leans closer, wrapping her arm around my shoulders. "Tell me what's going on. I'm a good listener, I promise."

It all comes spilling out. How Tagiz's family expects him to mate with someone else. How I tried to stay away from him and how the way he looks at me makes my heart beat so hard it feels like it'll fly out of my chest.

I wipe tears off my face. "Do you know what it's like to have Christmas on a different day when you're a kid? To know you can't celebrate on the *real* holiday because your father is with his *real* family? The mistress and the illegitimate kid don't get December 25. Or even the twenty-sixth. They get the twenty-seventh or the twenty-eighth."

Another tear slips down my cheek, and Beth grabs my hand. I let out a sob-laugh. "Why are *you* crying?"

She wipes her face, hunching her shoulders. "I can't help it," she mutters. "I'm ridiculous when my friends are hurting."

I smile at that. "You're a little empath." I sigh. "My mom was the other woman. I didn't figure it out until I was eight or nine and I heard her talking to my father. He may have loved my mother. May have loved me, even. But he was never going to leave his wife. Ever. By the time I was a teenager, Mom had finally accepted it, and I hated him more than anything in the world."

"I can't imagine how hard that was for you," Beth murmurs. "Did you have a relationship with him as an adult?"

I shake my head. "His wife wanted to move to California when I was a teenager. So they did. All of a sudden, he was gone, and I was the one who had to call 9-1-1 when my mother swallowed a bottle of pills. I was the one who had to watch as she broke and had to rebuild herself. You know she never took a cent of his money? She was owed child support at the very least. But she was too proud, and instead, she worked three jobs and died on the way to her night shift at the crappy diner down the road."

"You think what's going on with you and Tagiz is like your mom and dad?"

"Don't call him that," I snap and immediately regret it. I wrap my arm around Beth's shoulders. "I'm sorry."

"No, I get it. I wouldn't want to consider someone like that my dad either."

I sigh. "I watched her as I grew up. I saw how miserable she was, pining for someone else. How she pretended like December 25 was just another day. One year, I was so mad I opened all the presents under the tree on Christmas Day. The *real* Christmas Day. She cried for three hours."

Guilt buries itself deep in my stomach at the memory.

"You were just a kid." Beth's voice is gentle.

"Yeah. And he was celebrating Christmas with his real family. You know I have three brothers and a sister I've never met?" I let out a harsh laugh. "I guess I'll probably never meet them now."

"You know what I'm going to say," Beth murmurs.

"I know. I need to talk to Tagiz. He's going to break my heart, I know it."

Beth's jaw juts out, and her eyes turn steely. She may be gentle and kind, but she's also one hell of a fighter. "You know, I'm happier than I ever thought I could be. I have my mate and the little brat of a kid who makes me laugh until my stomach hurts even as he makes me want to pull my hair out in frustration—sometimes within the same few minutes. But I can tell you this: if I ever thought Zarix was going to be with another woman, even if he *wanted* to be with me, I'd leave so fast his head would spin."

I nod, winding my fingers together in my lap. "I shouldn't have slept with him. I was weak."

Beth sighs. "You were in love. It's different."

She laughs at the look on my face. "It's rare to find two people who fit together as well as you and Tagiz. But he's hurting you, Zoey. You need to tell him everything you told me. So he understands."

"I want him to choose *me*, Beth. But if he doesn't, I'm not going to hang around and watch him mate with someone else."

She nods. "I wouldn't either. As Nevada would say, fuck that shit."

I burst out laughing as she drags me to my feet, helping me collect the rest of my lunch.

"I'll clean this up," she says. "You need to talk to your man."

CHAPTER NINE

Z oey

I smile down at Harry, the karja. Yes, I named him. Yes, I know that was a stupid thing to do. He's not a pet. He's a wild animal. But I had to call him *something*.

"You don't even have a limp anymore. Is every creature on this planet a faster healer than us poor humans?"

He stretches up on his back paws and licks at my cheek, and I laugh.

"Are you hungry?"

He seems to perk up even more at that, and I get to my feet. I'll go get him some food, and then I'll go find Tagiz. After my talk earlier with Beth, I know I need to put all my cards on the table.

I bite my lip, wiping my sweaty palms on my dress. I don't know how to explain to him I need him to make a choice. I need him to choose *me*. But if he doesn't, I won't be hanging around to see him mate with Malis. I saw what it did to my mother to be second best. I'm worth more than that.

I'm so lost in thought I've walked past the food kradi. I turn to walk back, and my heart stutters in my chest.

Tagiz is holding Malis close as she murmurs to him. I take a moment to gaze at them, my chest clenching at how *right* they look together. Unlike me, her head brushes his chin, while I'm so small next to him that I probably look like a child.

My stomach twists. This situation isn't going to get any better. Tagiz hasn't said it, but it's clear his father will make him choose between his family and me.

If I had the chance to have my mom back, I'd jump at it. So how can I expect Tagiz to give up his family for me?

I attempt to blink back my tears, but they're already dripping down my face. I must make some kind of sound because Tagiz looks up, surprise on his face.

"Little healer..."

I wipe at my damp face, and the words pour from my mouth almost before I'm even aware of them. "I'm sorry, Tagiz. But I can't do this anymore."

Malis steps back from him, moving toward me, her face concerned. "You know it's not what it looks like, Zoey."

I nod, and more tears slip down my face. "I know. But I'm tired of feeling like the other woman. I know you guys are in a horrible situation, and I'm sorry for it, I really am. But I can't watch this happen anymore. And the thought of you mating?" My voice cracks, and Tagiz's face turns to stone.

"Don't do this, little healer. Don't leave me."

Somehow, this both breaks my heart and makes me want to slap him across the face.

"How can I leave you, Tagiz? I was never truly *with* you."

It hits me then. I love Tagiz. He's kind, and loyal, and

strong. He has a soft heart, hidden within that incredible chest of his. He was the first man to make me feel truly seen. The first to make me feel like I was special.

But I love myself more.

He opens his mouth, and I step back.

"It's okay. I just want you to be happy. Do whatever it is that makes you feel good, Tagiz. Live the life you want, and that will be enough for me."

"Zoey—"

I hold up my hand. "If you care about me at all, don't follow me."

***

Zoey

I'm staring out between the bars of the cage, my breath coming in shallow pants. I shudder, freezing, but the sweat on my face tells another story.

Fever.

It was to be expected, I guess. Untreated cracked or broken ribs make it difficult to breathe. Without painkillers, the inability to take a full breath leads to the collapse of the far ends of the lungs.

And that leads to pneumonia.

It's almost ironic. If my ribs had punctured a lung, at least my death might've been relatively quick.

Now all I can hope for is to get to see the sky one last time before I die.

Even if it's not the same sky I was born under.

Then Tagiz is there, his hands gentle as he picks me up. His eyes are soft, and he brushes the tangled hair off my face as he gazes down at me.

"I have you," he says.

But then Malis is there too. And they're holding each other. Looking so perfect together that a chunk of my heart breaks off right there, falling to my feet with a thump.

———

I jerk, lifting my hands to my face. Something is...licking me.

I'm crying. The little fluff ball has been licking my tears, one of his paws on my chest as he leans over.

"Were you trying to wake me up?" I murmur.

He growls at me, but it's not a threatening growl. It's more like he's berating me, and I laugh.

I sit up, wiping the tears—and fluff ball spit—off my face.

"Is it my imagination, or do you look even bigger already? I know it's a survival mechanism, but this is ridiculous."

Karja mamas don't tend to stick around and look after their babies for long, so they're forced to take on the world by themselves.

I know what it's like to suddenly be all alone in the world, without any warning.

I brush his furry little ears, and he allows it, a sound similar to a purr leaving his throat. I grin at him. I figured I shouldn't let him run wild through the camp until he's trained. But he hates the little pen I set up for him near the forest, and he cried until I rescued him, bringing him back to my kradi. I thought he'd prefer to be closer to the wild, but maybe he hated being able to see the world but not actually partake in what it has to offer.

I get it.

I roll out of bed, get dressed, and find some food for the little guy, sneaking him to one of the clearings near my kradi so he can do his business near a large white tree.

"You're a sweetheart," I murmur as I crouch beside him, and he licks my hand. He seems to be pretty content sleeping most of the day, but according to some of the warriors, the karja will be causing havoc soon though.

I glance around, careful to stay away from Tagiz. When it comes to him, I feel weak. The last thing I need is to see the hurt in his eyes again when he looks at me. If I don't work on building a wall around my heart, I'll be right back where I started.

I take the karja back to my kradi, and he snuggles into the little bed I made for him. Then I head to the training arena to see if any of the warriors are free to walk with me into the forest.

I grin at the camp's grumpiest warrior. "You're back!"

Hewex doesn't exactly grin back at me, but his scowl lessens slightly as he nods. "Let me guess," he says. "You need to find some bark and twigs."

I laugh. "Have some respect."

He snorts, and I'm careful to keep my eyes away from the training arena. I just caught sight of a familiar set of wide shoulders, and I instantly turn away. I don't think I can handle seeing Tagiz looking relaxed and happy while I feel like my heart has been ripped from my chest.

"I can't come with you today—I have a meeting with Rakiz. But Kroniz has just finished training." He calls over the other warrior, and I can instantly feel Tagiz's eyes on me. I keep my own gaze fastened on Kroniz's face, refusing to give in to the urge to look at the man who has caused me so much pain.

Turns out, sadness and rage are two sides of the same coin.

Kroniz grins, nodding as Hewex explains he can't hang around. I eye Hewex. Is he trying to fix me up with Kroniz?

Kroniz seems to realize I don't want to chat, and I get down to business as soon as we're in the forest. I've forgotten my basket, so I pull a handkerchief from my pocket as I search for the tiny green berries.

Not for the first time, I'm thankful we were rescued by the Braxians. If we were left alone, starving on this planet, we probably would have resorted to eating anything we could get our hands on and been dead within hours.

I find the bright-green maradoza berries, examining them with a clinical eye. Just a few of these berries could mean certain death.

I shudder at the thought, wrapping them in my handkerchief and carefully placing them in my pocket.

"Zoey?"

I turn. "Oh, hey, Nevada. What are you doing out here?"

She shrugs, and I notice two warriors trailing after her. Rakiz is taking no chances with his pregnant queen. They stop and talk with Kroniz, and I bend, looking for the leaves we use to make ortar.

"I wanted to take a walk. Can I give you a hand?"

"Sure. Help me pick a few of those dark-green leaves right there. The larger the leaf, the better."

She nods, getting to work, but she rubs her back with a wince, and I narrow my eyes at her.

"Are you okay?"

Nevada rolls her eyes. "I'm fine. Back pain seems to go hand in hand with pregnancy. The miracle of life ain't all that miraculous from where I'm standing." I laugh, and she changes the subject. "How are you doing with everything, Zo? Still drinking that awful tonic?"

I examine her face. She has a good color, and she's no longer wincing. The nurse in me wants to press her about the pain, but if there's one thing I know about Nevada, it's that she hates it when people fuss over her.

"I'm done with that, finally. You know, Moni reminds me of one of the charge nurses I used to work with. Her motto was 'do no harm but take no shit.'"

Nevada grins at me. "Moni is scary. I'm convinced she's at least a little psychic."

My eyes widen as she tells me about her friend Jack and how Moni passed on a message from him. Seemingly from beyond the grave.

"Whoa."

Nevada nods. "Yep."

"What's it like being pregnant here?" I ask, suddenly curious.

Nevada angles her head, wincing again.

"You know, I never thought I'd have kids." She glances away, looking as vulnerable as I've ever seen her. "My mom was a drunk, and I never knew my father. My brother took off as soon as he could. I have no idea what a healthy family looks like, Zo. What if I screw this kid up? I don't even know if I have any real maternal instinct."

I'm not used to this kind of talk from Nevada. She's one of the most self-assured people I've ever met. But I get it. Having a baby on an alien planet in the middle of a war? It's got to be hard. Doing it without any understanding of what a functional family looks like? Even harder.

I choose my words carefully.

"You know, I've been thinking about this recently. My mom died when I was nineteen. Before that, it was mostly just the two of us. I think every parent wonders if they'll screw their kid up. But no matter what happened in my life, I knew my mom was in my corner. I knew if the shit hit the fan, I could call her, and whatever problem I had, we'd figure it out together."

I blink back tears, and Nevada straightens, her face sympathetic as she wipes her own eyes.

"Goddamn hormones," she mutters, and I let out a wet laugh.

"I think that's the best thing you can give a child, Nevada. The knowledge you're on their team. That they're never alone and that when they need you, you'll be right there next to them, fighting beside them. And if there's one thing I know about the kick-ass woman who rescued me from the Voildi, it's that she'll be that person for her kid. You'll figure everything else out."

I don't know who is more shocked—me or Kroniz—as Nevada pulls me into her arms for a hug. Nevada is many things, but a hugger she is not. Kroniz's mouth drops open as I make eye contact with him over Nevada's shoulder, and the warriors next to him look just as shocked.

I feel a shudder run through Nevada, and I pull back as she winces.

"We need to get you back to camp," I murmur. I'm beginning to get concerned her back pain may actually be contractions.

She nods, her face suddenly pale, and we both turn toward the guards.

I scream, jumping in front of Nevada as the clearing erupts into violence.

CHAPTER TEN

T agiz

She left me.

And I can't blame her.

The female I'm obsessed with. The female I *need*, would never put up with anything less than everything from her male. Zoey may be gentle and kind, but she is also strong. She has a core of fire.

I advance toward Rakiz, desperate to replace the aching in my chest with a different kind of ache.

Our swords are on the ground, and we've devolved into fists. No other warriors are even pretending to train anymore, choosing instead to place bets on the outcome of our match.

I duck beneath Rakiz's fist only to lose my breath in a whoosh as his other hand slams into my stomach. I've seen that move before.

"You've been training with Vrex."

Rakiz grins at me, his teeth bloody, thanks to the elbow I just smashed into his face.

"The Assassin of Agron has much to teach us about combat."

I smile, leaping forward as if attempting to plow my fist into his gut. He dodges it, but my leg is already up, my foot slamming into his ribs.

Rakiz snarls, but his eyes hold appreciation. "You've been training too."

"Dexar has much to teach me."

The snarl turns into a scowl, and I almost laugh. The two tribe kings were once reluctant allies and are now friends. But that friendship is still fraught with competition and ego.

I grew up training with Rakiz. By now we know exactly how the other fights, which makes each fight more challenging.

I'm furious at my father, at myself, at the world. A fight with Rakiz is exactly what I need. I want to bruise and bleed until my outside matches my insides.

I lost her.

My little healer has given up on me. The female who never gives up on anything—even a wounded karja—has decided I am wasted effort.

Because I hurt her. And she knows I would likely hurt her further.

My head snaps back as Rakiz's fist cracks into my cheek.

The world turns gray, and Rakiz's eyes are no longer amused when I finally meet them again.

"If you can't concentrate while fighting, choose another activity."

Fury courses through my blood. I know Rakiz is goading me, but fury feels better than desolation and regret.

I growl, feeling my cheek split where his knuckles made contact with my skin. I feint with my right fist, then whirl, driving my knee into his gut as he dodges right.

He slumps just enough for me to hammer my elbow into the back of his head. The warriors surrounding us erupt, shouting encouragement—to both of us.

There are few things Braxians enjoy more than watching a good fight.

Rakiz drops to his knees but instantly jumps back up to his feet.

"You are fighting as if possessed," he notes. "Should I guess why?"

I ignore him. Rakiz is excellent at getting beneath his opponent's defenses—both physically and mentally.

"Aaah," he says when I don't reply. "This is about the human healer."

He smiles as he says it, and my blood turns to fire. I roar as I lunge at him, and his eyes are as hard as the smile that plays around his mouth.

My fault. Zoey's pain and sadness are my fault.

"Rakiz!"

We both turn as Beth appears, her face pale. Rakiz frowns at her, and she ignores the warriors who grumble, unhappy with the interruption of our fight.

"I was just in the healers' kradi. Moni says Zoey never returned when she went to collect plants in the forest." Beth hesitates for one moment and then firms her jaw. "Nevada went to meet her."

Rakiz's face drains of color before flushing a deep red, his whole body trembling with rage. I reach for my sword, and I'm running toward the forest before I even realize I'm moving. Behind me, Rakiz bellows orders at his men, and the camp jumps into action.

Zoey.

The thought of her terror drives me forward, and I reach the forest, roaring her name. Some of the human women are already here with their mates, all of whom are staying close to them, their eyes hard, swords in their hands.

Terex steps close, and I glance behind him at his pregnant mate. "You should take her back to camp."

"She won't leave until we know what happened to her friends, and I won't make her."

I frown at that, and he shakes his head.

"You still have no understanding of these human females."

I ignore him, and we spread out, searching for clues. Rakiz falls into step with me, his face a mask of fury.

We almost trip over the bodies.

I drop to my knees, shaking Kroniz as Rakiz and his men check Nevada's guards. He seems to be breathing, and I frown. I see no blood, no lump on his head, no reason for him to be unconscious.

A branch cracks behind us, and Ellie steps forward, her face gray. Terex holds her elbow, and it seems as if it is only his strength that keeps her on her feet.

"Check for a red mark," she murmurs. "Some kind of...burn."

Kroniz groans as I cut off his shirt, finding the red mark on his chest. I recognize this. This comes from the stick weapons the Dokhalls used in battle against us.

"They have Nevada. My pregnant mate." Rakiz's eyes meet mine, the devastation clear.

Ivy is out of breath as she reaches us. "They're both smart. Nevada may be pregnant, but she's still training. I'd bet on her against a Dokhall bastard any day. And Zoey..."

I meet her eyes, and she nods at me reassuringly.

"She's got this, Tagiz. We'll find both of them."

Rakiz gets to his feet and begins giving orders. Kroniz groans again, finally opening his eyes.

He frowns, obviously confused, and I fight not to roar at him for allowing Zoey to be taken.

"Dokhalls," he says, and I nod.

"Tell me what happened."

"They came out of nowhere. One of them must be dying. I ran him through. Check which direction he was heading in. Look for a trail of blood."

"How many of them were there?"

"Five. Likely four now. They wanted Nevada."

I growl. "They want to use her to blackmail Rakiz into giving them the ship."

Kroniz nods. "I'm sorry. They were here with no warning. They must have been planning this for some time. But there is no excuse for our failure."

Moni appears, her face drawn as she begins checking on the other warriors.

I stand. "We will find them."

Vrex and Ivy call out, drawing my attention to fresh drops of blood scattered on a fallen tree, while Rakiz finds a tiny, blunt knife on the ground in the opposite direction. Vrex leans close, keeping his voice hushed.

"Ivy says she has the impression the Dokhalls aren't used to being outdoors. They fell for our traps during the battle, and they are not experienced at covering up their own tracks."

Moni steps close to Rakiz and murmurs to him. He holds up the knife, and I examine the handle.

It's Zoey's knife.

She had to decide—take the knife with her and hope to use it or leave it as a sign for us to find them.

She's trusting us to save their lives. Even after we allowed them to be taken.

For a moment, my throat is so tight I can't speak, and my voice is hoarse as I struggle for control.

"We need to split up."

Vrex nods. "Ivy and I will go with Rakiz toward the east. You take some of the guards and go west. We'll divide everyone else we can spare and send them to canvass the area just in case the tracks are an attempt to distract us."

I don't hesitate, gesturing to Jozet, Makil, and Grez. Kroniz has managed to get to his feet, and while his steps are wobbly, he insists on joining us.

"We will set a fast pace," I say.

He nods. "I will keep up."

I don't argue, simply moving toward the east. We find more tracks, and I shudder at the thought of Zoey at the mercy of those who have none.

I will kill them all.

Zoey

I'm pretty sure Nevada is in real labor. She's leaning over, holding on to a tree and panting as one of the Dokhalls sneers at her, grabbing her arm in an attempt to make her move.

She strikes out with her fist, and he raises his stick. The sight makes my heart pound, and my mouth goes dry. He waves it threateningly, and Nevada ignores him, groaning.

He growls, pointing the stick at her, and Nevada's hand lashes out, faster than I could've imagined. She pulls the stick from his hand, slamming it into his head. The other

Dokhalls immediately advance on her, and I thrust my body between Nevada and them. They're not hitting a pregnant woman on my watch.

"Get out of the way, Zoey."

I ignore that. Out the corner of my eye, I can see a spark of blue light from the weapon in her hand as she advances on the Dokhalls, but the light quickly fades.

Nevada laughs bitterly. "I'm guessing you guys need the ship to charge these things. We noticed after the battle that the ones we took from you no longer seemed to work so well."

One of the Dokhalls snarls. "We will soon have our ship back, and you will be in our cage, your spawn sold as a slave, human whore."

Oh no, he didn't.

Nevada dodges around me, and this time, she throws the weapon like a spear, hitting the Dokhall straight in the face.

Blood flows from his flat nose like a river, and he lets out a sound remarkably close to a squeal. Nevada snorts and then groans, obviously struggling through another contraction.

One of the other Dokhalls steps close, and I lash out, aiming for his balls as he grabs my hair. He's too fast, and he shakes me, my scalp burning as Nevada holds on to a tree again, panting.

"I may not be able to kill you until after we have our ship, but I can kill this human to teach you a lesson."

I wince, my eyes hot as he pulls on my hair. Nevada nods, straightening, and her eyes are resolute as they meet mine.

"Fine."

We walk silently after that, surrounded by the Dokhalls. Nevada has to stop multiple times, and I count between her contractions, feeling the blood draining from my face.

Three minutes.

Three fucking minutes.

"Hurry up."

I scowl at the Dokhall, and he looks unimpressed. When Nevada starts walking again, she glances at me, and I can see the knowledge on her face.

She might be having this baby today. Her contractions seem too strong for Braxton-Hicks, but I won't know until I can examine her.

My hands begin to shake. I've helped deliver babies before, but never solo. I'm not an ob-gyn, or even a doctor, and I have none of the instruments I'd need to get Nevada through this.

Please, God, don't let it be the real thing. You took my mom away when I was nineteen. You let me be abducted by aliens and almost killed. You owe me.

We stop at a cave. By now, Nevada is damp with sweat. From the look of the cave, these Dokhalls have been planning this for some time. There's a collection of furs on one side, a pile of badly carved utensils next to them. Further back, a large, wooden bowl sits on the dirt floor, likely carved from a fallen tree. It's filled with water, and I'm suddenly desperately thirsty.

The Dokhalls push us toward the back of the cave, close to the water, but I don't dare reach for it. I bet they'd kill me before allowing me to give Nevada some water.

We sit with our backs against the cave wall, and Nevada closes her eyes, her knuckles turning white as she clenches her fists. The Dokhalls huddle close to the cave entrance, likely making more plans to ruin our lives.

"Listen to me," she gasps afterward, and I lean close. "If

this is the real thing, and I'm having this baby, you'll need to take it and run."

I squint at her, and she reaches out, burying her hand in the front of my dress as she pulls me close, eyes wild.

"I'll distract them. You do whatever it takes to get my baby to Rakiz. Promise me, Zoey."

"No. You're both making it through this."

She bares her teeth at me. "I saved your life, you bitch. Save my baby."

I smile as I reach out and push her hair off her face. "And you were worried about your maternal instinct. Listen to me. *Listen.* I'm going to make sure you get out of here. If I can't, I'll get the baby out and come back for you. So if it comes to that, and I end up hauling ass out of here with your newborn, don't do anything stupid in the meantime."

We're only a few miles from camp. These guys aren't planning to keep us hidden for long. They want to threaten Nevada's safety and get Rakiz under their control. It's not like they can post a ransom note. They need to be able to send someone back to negotiate.

And from the furious voices at the front of the cave, they're deciding who that unlucky guy will be right now.

Kroniz managed to gut one of the Dokhalls when they attacked. The wounded Dokhall trailed after us for a while before he was unable to move any longer, and his friends decided to use his blood as a distraction, taking us in the opposite direction before we circled back around.

I know the Braxians, and when they find the blunt knife I dropped, they'll immediately head in this direction. Nevada and I weren't exactly being careful not to disrupt the forest around us as we walked through it. Each time she leaned against a tree, clenching her teeth through a contraction, she made sure to leave that tree with a little less bark.

And I scuffed my shoes over every single fallen tree, kicked at leaves, and overturned rocks.

I know Tagiz too. And even with everything that has happened between us, I know he'll be coming for us.

"Maybe I shouldn't have dropped that knife," I murmur to Nevada. "It was too blunt to be much use, but maybe I should've kept it."

Nevada shakes her head. "After they switched paths, we had to leave some sign behind. I have a knife strapped to my thigh," she whispers. "But it's all I have. We need to take them by surprise."

I almost laugh. Of course Nevada has a weapon hidden beneath her dress.

"Okay," I say, blowing out a shaky breath as my mind races. "There are only four of them left. That little guy is clearly the runt of the litter, and it looks like they're sending him back to negotiate with Rakiz. That'll give us three."

Three armed Dokhalls against a woman in labor and me.

Great.

I examine the Dokhalls, searching for any signs of weakness as they argue. After Kroniz slid his sword into that Dokhall's abdomen, one of Nevada's guards managed to cut another Dokhall. That one is favoring his right arm as his left hangs by his side, red with blood.

The Dokhall who seems to be the leader has the longest horns, and they wind back from his face, glinting in the sunlight. He hands a piece of material to One Arm, and the Dokhall wraps it around his shoulder, tying it with his teeth.

The third Dokhall glances at us, and he glowers at me as we make eye contact. His nose is definitely broken, and it must be painful because he winces every time he talks.

Karma is a bitch.

CHAPTER ELEVEN

Z oey

The Dokhall they sent to negotiate with Rakiz hasn't come back.

It's been hours, and I'm starting to panic. Soon after she became tribe queen, Nevada taught some of the warriors how to track through the wilderness without using their noses—which they previously relied on when they were hunting Voildi. But there's no sign of any Braxians, and I'm not sure how they could've missed our tracks.

Nevada's face is scrunched in pain as she pants through another contraction.

She meets my eyes as soon as it's over. "My water just broke."

"Okay." My mouth goes dry. "We're going to get through this, Nevada. It's going to be okay."

She ignores that, her eyes drifting around the cave.

"I was so excited when I learned I was pregnant," she

murmurs. "I was scared, sure. But I pictured the day I'd give birth, how Rakiz would get to see his baby born. How we'd always keep our kid safe."

The Dokhalls begin to argue, muttering amongst themselves. They glance at me, and one of them scowls, gesturing for the other two to follow him closer to the cave's entrance.

I have to do something. I have a plan, but the only way it will work is if the Dokhalls decide they're thirsty.

If it's the only shot I have, I have to make it count. I reach into the folds of my dress, wrapping my fingers around the rag in my pocket, still holding the green berries I collected earlier.

They will regret taking us from our home; oh yes, they will.

Long Horns points to something outside, and I know I'm not going to get another chance.

My stomach swims, but I lunge forward, squeezing the berries and straining the green juice through the handkerchief.

I stare at the water, squeezing as hard as I can.

Do no harm.

I squeeze harder, pleased when the juice begins to dissolve. I sweep the handkerchief through the water, spreading more of the juice.

But take no shit.

I scooch back to Nevada. One Arm glances back at us, and I do my best to seem innocent. He scowls, and I carefully avoid looking at the bucket of water.

"Listen," I murmur to Nevada when her contraction is over. "I doubt they're going to offer us any water, but if they do, don't drink it, okay? Try not to even touch it."

Her eyes widen, her lips trembling with the hint of a smile before she tenses again, reaching for my hand.

"You sneaky bitch," she gasps out. "I knew you had it in you."

I manage a tiny smile. "Do you want me to examine you?"

She glances at the Dokhalls. "We need to know how dilated I am, don't we?"

"It doesn't have to happen now," I tell her. "But I should probably check soon."

She leans her head against the wall of the cave.

"Rakiz will come for us," she murmurs as her eyes slide closed. "He'll come."

***

Tagiz

I slice through the Dokhalls. Somewhere behind me, deep in the forest, Rakiz roars in fury.

These Dokhalls attacked with no warning. When we demanded to know where Nevada and Zoey were, they gave us blank looks. Obviously, the Dokhalls who managed to survive the battle have split into factions.

Unfortunately, this attack is preventing us from finding our females.

One of the Dokhalls darts close, his light-stick glowing blue. I dodge, but he makes contact. My entire body jolts, my hands going numb, and I drop my sword.

He grins, charging me, his stick held high.

His grin turns to dismay when the blue light disappears. I'm still unable to pick up my sword, so I lash out, kicking at him. My movements are clumsy as I recover from the jolt of his weapon, but I'm lucky, my foot catching him in the jaw.

Frustration courses through my body as another

Dokhall replaces him. I snarl as my arms tingle, finally working again, and this time I manage to swipe my sword off the ground before beheading the creature in one movement.

The ground shakes, and my ears ring as Rakiz's next roar is echoed by something much more dangerous.

Dragix.

Charlie is on his back, a long knife in her hand. The dragon swoops, blowing fire at the Dokhalls at the edge of the group attacking us.

They turn to ash.

Dragix banks, cutting through the sky as he turns for another dive.

Dokhalls scatter, screaming. I don't bother chasing them. Instead, I attempt to discern which direction Zoey and Nevada were taken. The attack has likely made it much more difficult for us to find them, the Dokhalls erasing any tracks.

I grind my teeth.

Kroniz reaches me. His color is slightly better, but he can barely meet my eyes, and I know he is filled with shame at his failure.

"There were no reports of Dokhalls in the area," I tell him. "Our sentries failed. Our guards failed—"

"And I failed."

My hands fist as I think of the karja, who warned us of a scent he didn't like in the forest. I planned to talk to Rakiz about it but hadn't yet found the time.

Because I was too busy figuring out how to get out of my mating with Malis.

"We all failed," I grind out.

"You were working with the information you had," Jozet says as he approaches us. "There was no way for you to know you should have been closer to the females."

Kroniz's jaw tightens. "I failed them. But I won't fail them again."

I survey the area as Dragix flies in Rakiz's direction.

Hewex arrives, out of breath after fighting alongside Rakiz's group.

"There is a small cave northeast of here," he murmurs, closing his eyes, and I know he's picturing a map of this area in his head. Few people know directions like Hewex. He has spent most of his life away from camp.

"A cave?" I attempt to picture it, and he opens his eyes with a nod.

"It's in what used to be Voildi territory. No Braxian would choose to go there unless they were specifically hunting any remaining Voildi in the area."

My stomach muscles clench. "If the Dokhalls have taken the females to the cave, any Voildi who still believe it is their territory may also attack."

"There is also another cave to the west," he says. "It's a karja's lair."

I tense. A karja in the wild will fight any who attempt to claim its territory. If it's full-grown, we will need to be on our guard.

"What else?"

He closes his eyes again. "If we continue north, we will be heading toward the Colossal Water."

I don't believe the Dokhalls can travel across the water, but I remember the sentry telling Rakiz they were seen speaking with the Zintas. Could this kidnapping be part of some larger plan?

I glance at Jozet. "Send one of the younger warriors back to Rakiz. Tell him we are moving north."

Zoey

I watch out of half-closed eyes as the Dokhall with the broken nose takes a cup of water.

Maradoza berries taste bitter, but the Dokhall doesn't seem to notice, guzzling the water down and dipping his cup for more.

I chew on my lip. Maybe I didn't squeeze enough juice into the water?

There's nothing I can do about it—it's not like I have any more berries to add.

One Arm follows him into the cave, muttering about the Dokhall that left earlier. He still hasn't returned, and it seems as if their plans are now falling apart.

That's what you get, motherfuckers.

Nevada clenches my hand, and my heart aches at the pain and fear on her face. Labor is the most vulnerable time in a woman's life, and if the warriors don't find us soon, Nevada might be giving birth in a cave.

One Arm follows his friend's lead, drinking a cup of water. He doesn't take any more, and I chew on my lip. I only had a few berries, and there was a lot of water. I need them to at least fall unconscious, although honestly, I wouldn't be all that upset if they fell over and died.

Nevada groans again.

"Be quiet," One Arm says.

I glare at him. "She's in labor, asshole."

I turn back to Nevada, and I don't see his fist coming. It slams into the side of my head, and fireworks appear in front of my eyes.

"Zoey," Nevada gasps, and I take a moment, wrestling with the pain that explodes through my brain.

"I'm okay."

The Dokhall sneers at me, walks back to the front of the cave, and sits down, waiting.

Long Horns is clearly enraged, pacing back and forth in front of the cave entrance, shooting Nevada and me furious looks. If he didn't need us, I have no doubt we'd already be dead.

Where are you, Tagiz?

I'm not allowing myself to imagine the worst. That this was part of some bigger attack and Tagiz is lying somewhere, dead.

"Where the hell is Rakiz?" Nevada growls. "I'm going to kick his ass when I see him next."

I laugh softly at that, and Broken Nose glowers at me from where he's leaning against the cave wall.

Do his eyes look blurry? He blinks, and my heart stutters in my chest as it takes him a second to reopen his eyes.

Nevada lets out a wail, and Long Horns glowers, stepping back into the cave.

That's when Broken Nose slumps to the ground.

"Zoey," Nevada gasps, hunched over. "Reach under my dress and hand me my knife. Cover my body so they can't see."

Long Horns is standing in front of his friend, nudging him with his foot. One Arm steps toward him and stumbles, his brow furrowed in confusion.

I shove Nevada's dress up, my hand searching for the hilt of the knife. I grab it, passing it to her, and One Arm drops to his knees.

Long Horns narrows his eyes at his friend as he loses consciousness, and my hands begin to shake as he swings his head, eyes focused on us.

"What did you do?" he snarls.

He stalks over to us, grabbing me by the front of my

dress and hauling me up to my knees. In a perfect moment of unity, I reach back as Nevada slides the handle of the knife into my hand.

Long Horns shakes me, and I gasp. He raises his fist, and I swing my arm wildly.

Surprise is on my side.

Blood sprays my face as I slash the knife across his throat. I may not know much about self-defense, but I sure as hell know where the carotid artery is in humans. And it looks like Dokhalls have a large artery in a similar spot.

He drops me, gurgling as he clutches at his throat. It's not pretty, and my stomach is swimming as he falls to the ground.

"Holy shit, Zo. Remind me never to piss you off."

I swallow down bile. I've never killed anyone before. I don't know if the other Dokhalls are dead, but I get to my feet, still clutching the knife in my hand.

Nevada is silent as I step close to One Arm. I hesitate, my heart pounding. If he's conscious, this could be the last move I make.

Nevada groans, the sound more like a sob, and a surge of protectiveness makes the decision for me.

I lean down and slice his throat.

Broken Nose is already dead, his mouth covered in foam. I step over him, my movements mechanical, my body numb. Am I in shock?

Nevada gets to her feet, leaning against the cave wall as she rocks from side to side. I move further out of the cave, throw my head back, and scream as loud as I can.

I continue until I'm hoarse, and Nevada nods approvingly.

"You're not worried about more Dokhalls?" I ask her.

"We're close enough to camp that if the Braxians are

looking for us, surely someone will have heard that. Besides, if the Dokhalls get here first, maybe you can offer them some water."

I narrow my eyes at her. "Ha ha."

She grins and then clenches her eyes shut, moaning. I rub her lower back, and she leans into my hands.

"That helps," she says.

"I need to examine you. I'm not going to touch you until I can wash my hands, but I need to see what's going on. Is that okay?"

She nods, and I help her sit back down against the cave wall.

Nevada has had her bloody show. And within a few minutes, she's no longer interested in talking between contractions. I go outside again and scream some more.

I have my head tipped back, the knife clutched in my hand, and I'm screaming furiously at the sky when Tagiz and Hewex burst through the trees, a group of warriors behind them.

I take one look at Tagiz and burst into tears.

He grabs me, pulling me close. Behind him, Hewex checks the Dokhalls, glancing from the Dokhalls to the knife in my hand, and his eyes widen slightly.

Tagiz's huge hands cup my face, and suddenly I'm gasping into his mouth as he *devours* me.

His lips are hot and hard, and one of his hands slides to my back, pulling me even closer. I tilt my head sideways, and he plunders my mouth, not holding back this time.

I revel in it.

The tiniest moan leaves my throat, and it's that sound of pure *want* that shakes me from my daze.

I push away from Tagiz, trembling. "Where's Rakiz?"

He opens his mouth, his eyes dark as he begins to

explain something about another attack, but Nevada calls my name.

I glance back at the cave. "We can't move her without a mishua. Send someone for Rakiz."

Tagiz nods and turns to one of the warriors. "Run," he says, and the guy sprints back in the direction they came from.

"I'm scared more of them will come."

"We have Kroniz and some of the other warriors guarding the perimeter."

Relief rushes through me. "Okay. I need you guys to boil some water," I tell Tagiz.

He glances at Jozet, who is staring at the cave, horror on his face as Nevada groans in pain.

I elbow Jozet. "Water. Now."

He gets to work, gathering sticks for the fire, and I head back into the cave.

Nevada opens her eyes, squinting at Tagiz.

"Rakiz?" she pants.

"He's coming," I say. "It's going to be okay."

I glance at Tagiz. "Tell me they're bringing a healer."

"Moni was with Rakiz. We were all separated during the attack. Dragix arrived and handled the Dokhalls we were fighting, and he was circling back toward Rakiz when we left."

Nevada gets onto her hands and knees, a long groan leaving her throat. Tagiz's face turns white.

Jozet approaches. He's managed to find another bowl from the sad collection of utensils in the corner. The Dokhalls must have been here for at least a few days. Maybe even longer.

Steam is rising from the bowl, and I smile at him.

"Place it right there, please. I need some string, a knife

that hasn't been used to kill anyone recently, and the cleanest, warmest shirt we have."

The guys get to work, murmuring amongst themselves, and I turn to Nevada, who is currently in her own little world, dealing with the pain.

I examine her, and my chest fills with dread, although I manage to keep my voice light, confident.

"Okay, Vada. Soon, you'll probably get the urge to push. Wait until you can't do anything *but* push, and then you'll give it all you've got."

She nods, and I take some of the clean water, giving her a few sips. I rip the sleeve off my dress and bathe her face.

Jozet's eyes are wild when I glance at the warriors, and Tagiz still looks pale. They have no problem slaughtering any creatures who threaten us, but the sight of a woman in labor has stunned them into terrified silence.

Jozet breaks that silence as Nevada lets out a sound of such agony that my heart flips in sympathy. "Rakiz needs to be here."

"Well, he isn't. Pass me that shirt."

"She can't die without him."

I swing my head so fast I'm surprised I don't get whiplash. "*Excuse me?*"

Nevada stares at him, her face creased in exhaustion as she recovers from her last contraction. "You think I'm going to die?"

"The baby..." His voice trails off as he glances between Nevada and me. Then he seems to get some courage from somewhere because his jaw tightens. "The-The size of the baby. Human females cannot birth it."

I don't think I've ever seen this kind of fear in Nevada's eyes before, and the sight makes me tremble with rage as I get to my feet.

"Get out."

"But—"

I point to the entrance. "Stand there, guard us, and don't say another fucking word."

I narrow my eyes at Tagiz as Nevada lets out a sound that reminds me of a wounded animal.

It's followed by a masculine roar. "Nevada!"

Oh, thank God. Rakiz runs into the cave, his eyes wild as he reaches for his mate. Nevada is in the middle of a contraction, and she slaps his hands away as he attempts to cup her face.

"Give her a moment," I murmur. "Where's Moni?"

"We had to send the healers back when we were attacked. She's on the way now."

Nevada reaches for Rakiz's hand, panting. "I knew you'd get here. I knew you'd make it. If I die, you have to tell the baby all about me. Teach them to be brave and strong but to ask for help when they need it. Teach them about family and friendship and tell them their mama loved them more than anything in the world."

Rakiz's face pales. "You're not dying." His eyes are wild when they meet mine. "Tell her she's not dying."

I throw my hands up into the air. "For the love of God, enough with the dramatics," I say, keeping my voice light. "Women have been birthing babies—even huge babies—for thousands of years."

Nevada ignores that. "Promise."

"I promise," he says, and then his eyes meet mine again, and my chest aches at the sight of our tribe king filled with fear.

CHAPTER TWELVE

T agiz

"I need to push," Nevada says.

"Go ahead," Zoey replies, her voice calm. But I know the little healer better than anyone else. I have studied her expressions, her body language, the tilt of her head, everything about her since the moment I first laid eyes on her.

She is not calm. Not at all.

She rinses her hands in the water, scrubbing them over and over.

Nevada clutches at Rakiz, pushes him away, and then pulls him close again, wailing. "You did this to me, you bastard. If I die, I'm going to haunt you forever."

Rakiz leans over and presses a kiss to her forehead. "I would welcome your presence any way I could have it, karja, but you will not die. You would not leave our baby without a mother."

I move closer to the cave entrance in an attempt to give

them more privacy, but I can't help but be fascinated by the way my tiny healer takes control. She directs Rakiz into position until he is sitting behind Nevada.

At one point, Zoey glances at me and orders more water, and I relay the instruction to Jozet, who jumps into action, his shoulders still hunched in shame.

Nevada vomits, noisily, and Zoey declares it "perfectly normal," gently wiping her mouth.

Jozet arrives with more water.

"I saw Moni through the trees," he says.

"Oh, thank God," Zoey murmurs, her eyes still on Nevada as she pushes.

"Don't leave me," Nevada groans.

"I won't. I promise."

Nevada screams a curse, and Rakiz flinches. His eyes meet mine for a long moment, and I can see the regret.

He knows this was a mistake.

Zoey raises her voice, drawing Nevada's attention. "Mouth closed, Vada. If you're yelling, the energy is going out of the wrong hole."

Nevada manages to choke out a laugh. "I hate you."

"I know. The head is almost out. Push."

Nevada pants. "I can't do this."

"Look at me. At me. You only have a few more pushes and you'll get to meet your baby. You *can* do this. I promise."

Nevada shakes her head, but then she lets out a scream that's filled with so much pain that I instinctively move closer, wishing I could do something...anything to help.

"What do you need?" I ask Zoey.

She glances at me, wincing in sympathy as she murmurs something about a "ring of fire." "More water."

I jump into action, striding out of the cave, and it's not until I return that I realize there are still two full bowls of water next to her. Zoey is clearly just trying to keep us busy.

Rakiz's eyes meet mine, and I know he feels even more useless than I do.

Zoey glances at me. "I need that sharp knife. Boil it in water and bring it to me."

I do as she says, and as soon as I return, Moni comes bustling in.

She kneels next to Zoey between Nevada's legs, nodding approvingly at whatever she sees.

Zoey glances up at me. "Hold the knife and don't let anything touch the blade."

I nod, moving next to Rakiz. From here, I can see Zoey's face, her brow furrowed in concentration.

"The head is out, Nevada," she says, her voice low, encouraging. "I can see a beautiful head of hair. It's just the shoulders now. One more push and your baby is here."

I glance down at Nevada's face. I don't think I've ever seen anyone look so exhausted before.

Rakiz nuzzles her hair. "You can do it, karja. Let's meet our child."

One more howl, and Moni and Zoey jump into action. Within moments, Zoey is holding a tiny creature, one of her fingers gently stroking its nose. She takes Jozet's shirt and uses it to vigorously rub the baby's back until it lets out a wail that makes everyone smile in relief.

Zoey's eyes are damp as she grins up at Nevada. "You have a baby girl."

Rakiz takes the knife from me, slicing through something long and coiled that makes my stomach roll. Then the baby is placed on Nevada's chest, and Rakiz is beaming, eyes lit in pure joy as he presses kisses to both their heads.

Zoey rinses her hands. "You did great. Just the placenta to go. Not long now and we can get the hell out of here."

Nevada laughs, and it seems as if she's glowing from within as she gently strokes her daughter's head. "Thank you, Aunty Zoey."

Now that the worst seems to be over, I join Jozet outside, and we both watch as warriors bring mishua to the cave entrance, one of them with a cart attached for Nevada and the baby.

Hewex approaches from where he has been stalking through the trees, looking for any Dokhalls who dare approach.

The sun is beginning to go down when Nevada is finally loaded into the cart. Rakiz is still beaming at his family, and I attempt to ignore the way my chest tightens as I shift my attention from him to Zoey.

She's striding toward us, and she doesn't look happy.

"Uh-oh," Jozet says.

Zoey scowls at him as she reaches us. "What the fuck was that?"

He stares at the ground. "I'm sorry."

"You should be. In what world do you live in where it could possibly be a good idea to suggest a pregnant woman is going to die while that woman is in labor and without the father of her baby?"

He's silent, and she shakes her head, obviously exasperated.

"Where did you get this idea?"

I clear my throat. "He heard it from my father."

She snorts. "And what would Calix know?"

"Braxians have large babies. Human women are small."

"Small and tough," she snaps.

Jozet and I both nod, and Zoey throws up her hands. "We'll talk about this later," she promises, stalking away.

Something about watching my little healer order around warriors twice her size makes me hard as stone.

But it has always been this way. From the moment I saw her curled up in that cage, it was like recognizing the other half of my soul. Her eyes were slits as she glared at me as if daring me to approach, exhaustion and pain clear on her face. I knew, looking at the tiny female who was so close to breaking but still fighting...I knew she was *mine.*

I push the thought away for now and focus on getting ready to guard Nevada and the baby.

Nevada is sitting in the cart, while Rakiz orders everyone into position. He's now tense, his brow creased as he glowers around him, and it's easy to understand why.

If the Dokhalls are planning another attack, now would be the perfect time to do it.

Zoey

We're all on edge, wondering if there will be another attack, but thankfully, the trip back to camp is uneventful.

The ground is littered with burned Dokhall bodies in one clearing as we pass, and smoke drifts toward us on the wind. At one point, a ground-shuddering roar sounds from deep within the forest, and Nevada smiles down at her daughter.

"Uncle Dragix is unhappy," she murmurs.

I laugh.

I will forever remember the terror of the walk from our

camp to that cave, but it feels like it only takes us moments to travel back as I sit in the cart with Nevada.

Her daughter is still lying against her skin on her chest, a heap of warriors' shirts wrapped around them both to keep them warm.

As soon as we arrive back at camp, it erupts in celebration, cheers sounding from all directions as the cart rolls through the kradis.

Nevada smiles, and Rakiz's chest puffs up with pride. He gently lifts Nevada into his arms before carrying her and the baby into the tashiv. Moni follows them in to give Nevada one last checkup and to make sure the baby latches, and I jolt as Tagiz takes my elbow.

I blink. I'm still standing outside, staring at the tashiv, my mind a hundred miles away.

Tagiz releases me for a moment and speaks to one of the servants, who glances at me and nods, rushing away. He returns to my side, stroking some of my hair back off my face.

"You need to rest," he says gruffly.

I nod. I'm so tired I feel like I'm practically sleepwalking, the adrenaline crash hitting me hard.

"Let me just check in on Nevada. I want to make sure she doesn't need anything."

He nods and waits by the door. Nevada smiles at me from her bed. Arana is standing near the bathing room, overseeing the filling of the bath as she beams at Nevada.

"How are you feeling?" I ask.

"Completely in love," she murmurs.

The baby lets out a tiny squeak, and I lean over.

"She latched okay?"

"Yes, thank God. And Moni said I didn't even need any

stitches. As far as cave births go, I'm calling this one a success."

I sigh. "Let's never do that again."

She laughs. "Thank you, Zoey. I know I've said it before, but I couldn't have gotten through it without you."

"Yes, you could've." I smile. "You probably would've killed all those Dokhalls while birthing that beautiful baby."

She grins at me, and I lean over, stroking her daughter's soft, little head.

In the other room, Rakiz is throwing out orders, pacing as he speaks to a group of warriors.

"Do you want to hold her?" Nevada offers.

I hold out my arms. "Gimme."

Now that she's all cleaned up, and I'm not responsible for bringing her into the world, I can simply enjoy a snuggle.

"God, she's so small."

Nevada smirks. "She didn't feel all that small coming out. My coochie will never be the same."

"Your poor mommy," I murmur to the baby. "That's the price we women pay." I return my attention to Nevada. "Do you know what you're going to call her?"

Nevada's gaze is full of love as I stroke her daughter's soft cheek, inhaling that newborn baby smell.

"We're still thinking about it."

Rakiz steps into the room, his gaze immediately flying to Nevada's face before shifting to his daughter.

"I'm going to let you guys rest," I say. "Let me know if you need anything. I'm sure the whole camp will be begging to babysit, but I'm first in line."

Rakiz smiles at me, taking the baby from my arms. He holds his daughter as if he has been doing it his whole life, and she's tiny in his huge hand. He wraps his other arm around me, and it's clear he's giddy with happiness.

"Thank you," he murmurs, and I grin up at him.

"You're welcome."

I walk out into the dark night, the air cool on my skin. Surprisingly, Tagiz is still waiting, leaning against the tashiv as he gazes up at the stars.

"You were incredible today, little healer," he says as his eyes meet mine.

"It was a team effort."

"I saw what you did to the Dokhalls," he says. "How?"

"I poisoned them," I murmur. That's something I'll need to deal with. I don't regret it, but I'm a nurse. I'm used to saving lives, not taking them.

Tagiz's eyes widen slightly before pride flashes through them.

"You kept yourself and the tribe queen safe," he says. He places one hand at my lower back as he walks me to my kradi.

"Thank you for coming for us."

He frowns at me. "I may not be able to give you what you need, but I will always come for you, little healer."

Stop calling me that, I want to beg. *Stop giving me nicknames and making me wish for things I can't have.*

My eyes burn. I'm just tired. Once I have a good night's sleep, I'll be able to function again.

I turn to him as we reach my kradi, gazing up at his face. His jaw is hard, and his eyes...they look...sad.

Well, I'm fucking sad too.

Tagiz's hand comes up, and for a moment, I think he might kiss me. Instead, he strokes one finger along my jaw, gazing down into my eyes.

"Good night, Zoey," he says, turning and walking away.

I whirl, stalking into my kradi, and freeze as I find my bath full of clean water, steam still rising into the air.

He had someone fill my bath for me.

I strip off my clothes, slide into the bath, and dunk my entire head beneath the water.

If some of the drops of water rolling down my face taste like salt, that's no one's business but mine.

CHAPTER THIRTEEN

Zoey

I feel drained when I wake to the fur ball licking at my face. Although, I don't know if I can call him a fur ball anymore now that he's growing so fast.

"You know, this wake-up method is gross and unnecessary."

He opens his mouth, displaying a row of sharp teeth, and I roll my eyes. "You can't intimidate me. I'm friends with a dragon."

The karja is beginning to roam further from my kradi. I was concerned until I spoke to Tagiz about it, and he said once a karja is tamed, it does not hunt close to home. Apparently, the people in this camp are safer for having the karja around, since he'll now protect what he considers his territory with his life.

I let the karja loose in the forest. Now that he's no longer limping and his ribs are no longer sticking out, I don't worry about him being prey for a larger animal. He'll go hunt his own breakfast and return to my kradi to sleep when he's done.

I didn't wake up in time for my training with Kroniz, but something tells me he'll give me a pass after everything that happened yesterday. Still, I want to make sure he knows I'm on for our next session, so I head to the training arena to see if he's there.

"Ah." He grins when he sees me. "Your name is on everyone's lips this morning. I'm free to train you tomorrow, although from what I heard about your actions in that cave, I'm not sure you need it." He winks, and I blush.

"I just did my job," I murmur, and his face turns serious.

"From where I'm standing, it sounds like you used your particular skills and strengths to save the day. Not all battles are won on the battlefield. There's a reason strategy is so important."

I open my mouth, unsure what to say. A wind kicks up, and we both turn our attention to the sky as a shadow blocks out the sun.

Dragix's huge form is all I can see in the sky, and Charlie waves at me from his back. Warriors scatter, but I stay where I am. I've seen Dragix land a hundred times by now, and he has an incredible ability to aim for the tiniest space. He won't crush anyone. Unless he chooses to.

Charlie is off his back as soon as he lands, and she runs at me, giving me a hug.

"I heard what happened," she says. Behind her, Dragix shifts into his human form, although he'd likely snarl at me if he heard me refer to it that way. Dragix is many things, but he'll never be human.

I avert my gaze as the dragon is suddenly naked, stalking across the training arena toward us as if he doesn't have a care in the world.

Charlie pulls back, eyeing me.

"Yeah, it was crazy," I admit. "No one saw it coming. We've been expecting the Dokhalls to attack en masse like they did last time. But it seems they've broken into smaller groups, which means they're likely even more dangerous."

Charlie sighs. "Dragix has been hunting them. They're smart, but he must've taken out a hundred of them yesterday."

Dragix reaches us, wrapping his arm around Charlie. Pure devotion shines in those gold eyes as he looks at her, and then he nods at me.

"I will go speak with Rakiz," he says.

"I packed you some pants." Charlie holds up the bag she's clutching in her fist, and he scowls but takes it, walking away.

"He's not the biggest fan of clothes," Charlie murmurs.

"With a body like that, I don't blame him." I slap a hand over my mouth. "Sorry."

She throws her head back, cracking up. "Girl, it is what it is."

I grin at her. "What are you guys doing here anyway? I thought you were hanging out on your mountain for a while."

"We were. But with everything that's happening, Dragix is beginning to get nervous I'll be taken. He's a threat to anyone he decides is his enemy on this planet, and if the Dokhalls have been studying him enough, they'll know all they need to do to get him to fall in line is threaten me—just like they attempted to do to Rakiz. So I'm going to stay here while Dragix goes hunting."

"Well, I can't say I'm disappointed to have you around. Beth and Alexis are staying for a while too."

Charlie nods with a smile, linking her arm through

mine. But her expression says her mind is clearly elsewhere, and I narrow my eyes at her.

"What's wrong?"

"Nothing."

I tilt my head, and she glances around us before a deep sigh leaves her. "I'm pretty sure I'm pregnant."

I bounce, throwing my arms around her. "Oh my God. I'm so happy for you!"

Her smile is small, and I freeze.

"This is a good thing, right?"

"Oh yes. Of course. I mean, I never thought I'd have kids, but then I never imagined I'd meet someone like Dragix. And he's the last of his kind. I know he loves the idea of having a family."

"So what's going on?"

"I haven't told Dragix yet."

"Uh-huh. Why?"

She smiles at that. "There's no way he'll leave me behind to go hunt the Dokhalls. It's still so early. This is my first missed period, and we both know how these things can go. I don't want to distract him until I know for sure."

I nod. "I get it. I think you should tell him soon though."

"I will. I just want to be certain. I don't want to get his hopes up. And there's no point distracting him from his revenge plans unless I'm sure. Anyway, thanks for listening."

"Anytime."

"So give me the deets. I know all about Nevada's cave baby, which is what I'm calling her until Nevada punches me," she says, and I laugh. "But what exactly happened with Vivian and Sarissa?"

I fill her in, and her mouth drops open as we arrive in front of Nevada and Rakiz's tashiv.

"Holy shit. So they're just going to stay there?" She frowns. "I don't like it."

"Neither do I. I want us to all be together." I nod toward a group of the human women who landed with the last ship as they walk toward the training arena. "It was difficult explaining the decision to those guys. It sounds like Sarissa was the one holding everyone together on that ship."

"God. Logically, I know it makes sense, but…"

"Yeah. You should've seen that marketplace though. I had no idea there were people on Agron trading with other planets. This could really be our opportunity to get out of here."

Charlie angles her head, her gaze steady on my face. "And you're sure you want to take that opportunity?"

I sigh. "I don't know. I want that opportunity to exist though. For the other women, if not for me. And I can't deny I miss my life on Earth."

"And Tagiz?"

"Well…"

"Are you two going to stand outside my house and gossip all day? Or are you going to come in and see my daughter?" Nevada is standing in the doorway, hands on her hips.

Charlie bursts out laughing. "I was giving you a chance to have some time to yourself."

Nevada rolls her eyes. "Tribe queen, y'all. There *is* no time to myself. I accepted that when I took this gig. Get in here."

We follow Nevada inside her tashiv, finding she's entirely right. Rakiz is having a serious conversation with Dragix, Tagiz, and Terex in the main room, their voices hushed.

Tagiz's gaze finds mine as I walk in, and he scans my body, his eyes warm. I nod at him, pretending my heart doesn't break a little more every time I see him.

Dragix says something to Tagiz, drawing his attention, as we follow Nevada back into her bedroom.

Ellie is sitting near the bed, the baby in her arms. She beams at us as we walk in.

"Isn't she adorable?" Her voice is hushed, and Charlie practically trips over her feet as she bounces over to the baby.

"Naaaw. Good work, mama."

Nevada smiles, sitting on the edge of her bed. "I couldn't have done it without Zoey." Her smile turns into a smirk as she glances at me. "Maybe you should consider a career as the camp midwife."

I shudder at the thought. "No, thank you. I'll leave that business to Moni. Give me an amputated arm over a fully dilated cervix any day."

The other women crack up, and the baby opens her eyes, a tiny cry escaping her lips.

"Someone's hungry," Nevada says, holding out her arms. She pulls up her shirt, positioning the baby at her breast, and she immediately quiets.

"Did you get much sleep last night?" I ask.

"Nope. Rakiz is going to kick everyone out soon so I can nap. He's instituting a new rule—no meetings in our tashiv. He's going to use a kradi instead while we figure out what our new sleep schedule is going to look like."

Charlie plunks herself down on the bed next to Nevada, and I lean against the wall.

"Have you named her yet?" Charlie asks.

"Yep." Nevada grins. "Meet Danica. It was my grandmother's name. I never met her, but it means 'morning star.' After everything we've been through, it seemed fitting."

Ellie brushes away a tear as she smiles at them both. "It's beautiful, Nevada."

I nod. "I love it."

Rakiz pokes his head in the door. "They're leaving now, karja."

Charlie gets to her feet. "We'll let you get some rest."

Charlie leaves us outside the tashiv, murmuring something about talking to Blair—one of the new women. Apparently they've bonded, and they seem to have a lot in common.

Ellie hesitates as we watch Charlie stride away. She opens her mouth as if she has something to say and then clamps it shut again.

"What's going on, Ellie?"

"It's okay. You've got a lot going on. I know you're having...issues with Tagiz. I can wait a few days."

Her face is pale, and her hands are shaking.

I frown. "What's wrong? Is it the baby?"

Ellie got pregnant before Nevada, so I'm guessing she'll be due any day.

This is obviously the wrong thing to say because Ellie bites her lip, her eyes filling with tears.

"That's it," I say. "You're telling me what's going on."

I lead Ellie to the small clearing where the kids like to play. We take a seat, and I focus all my attention on her.

Ellie's face is so pale that I scan the clearing, wondering where Terex is. He's usually close by, unwilling to leave her side with everything that's going on. Most days, she watches him train and then they spend the rest of the day practically glued together.

From the way she's staring down at the ground, this isn't a conversation she wanted Terex to overhear.

"Okay," I say. "Tell me everything."

"I know I'm being stupid, but I'm terrified, Zoey."

"Terrified of childbirth?"

She sighs. "I just feel like it's not possible to be this happy without consequences. I know we're basically at war right now, and there are so many external things to focus on, but I never imagined I'd find someone I love as much as Terex. Sometimes I wake up, and the way he looks at me...I feel like I'm dreaming, you know?"

I tamp down the envy that wraps around my heart, cutting into it like barbed wire. "You're waiting for the other shoe to drop."

Ellie nods. "I guess I am. I just have this feeling it's all about to go terribly wrong." Her eyes fill with tears, and I reach for her hand.

"It's normal to be a little nervous."

She shakes her head. "I'm not a little nervous, Zoey. I'm pretty sure I'm going to die."

Where is this coming from? I frown. "I'm going to tell you the same thing I told Nevada when she was panicking. Women have been giving birth for thousands of years."

"Human women haven't been giving birth to Braxian babies!"

I blink at that. "You're right. But look at Nevada and Danica. Don't they help put some of your fears to rest?"

She sniffles and wipes away a tear. "Moni said Danica came a little early. My baby is bigger. I don't think I'm going to live through it."

I stare at her, stunned. "Let's back up a bit. Did Moni say something to make you worry? Where did you get this idea from?"

"It was a few weeks ago, I guess. I heard some of the warriors talking. They were convinced Nevada was going to die. I didn't say anything, but I barely slept. All I could think about was that poor baby without a mother. And Rakiz—" Her voice cracks.

"What the hell would Braxian warriors know about pregnant human women?"

I'm furious now. After Jozet's comments in the cave and Tagiz's admission about his father, I'm pretty sure I know where these rumors came from.

Ellie is the sweetest, kindest woman I know. She never has a bad word to say about anyone. And she deserves her happily ever after.

"If I die...I need you to promise you'll be there for Terex and the baby. Terex will be lost, Zoey. I need you to make sure he's okay."

"Ellie. You're not going to die." She stares at me, her lower lip trembling as she waits, and I sigh. "I promise. But listen, you can't think like that."

"Will you be there when I give birth?"

"Of course. If I can deal with Nevada in labor, I can deal with you." I'm rewarded with a tiny giggle.

I leave Ellie looking a little happier as she watches some of the tribe kids play on the grass.

Fury blinds me, and my body suddenly feels like it's on fire.

Enough is enough. It's time to meet Tagiz's dad.

CHAPTER FOURTEEN

T agiz

I'm sitting inside my parents' kradi while my father paces, shooting me occasional furious looks.

"I don't understand why you and Malis insist on waiting. You know each other well enough by now."

"It's not about how well we know each other, Father."

He growls at that. "What about your duty to your family, Tagiz?"

It takes all my self-control not to flinch, and he narrows his eyes at me, sensing weakness.

This is it. No longer will I pretend my need for my little healer does not matter.

"You!"

My head twists on my neck so fast I hear a crack, but I ignore it as Zoey strides toward us, her face flushed, hands fisted.

I expect her to come to me. Obviously it is *I* who has made the tiny healer this incensed.

But no, she stalks toward my father, a sneer I've never seen before on her beautiful face. Her beautiful *bruised* face, thanks to the vicious Dokhall who hit her yesterday.

"And who are you?" my father demands.

I sigh. My father knows the human females by now. They have been here for long enough that gossip about each of them has swept through the camp. Most of the warriors even know the names of the new females who came on the last ship, and many are attempting to convince them to mate with them.

"I'm the woman who delivered the tribe queen's baby. The woman who just had to comfort my friend who was crying, terrified of giving birth thanks to your vicious rumors."

Surprise flashes through my father's eyes, but it's quickly replaced by an icy fury I know well.

"They're not rumors," he snaps. "Human females are weak. Too weak to mate with our warriors." He waves his hand toward where I'm sitting, and Zoey doesn't even look at me. My stomach clenches.

"Let me be very clear," she murmurs. "If I ever hear you have been spreading rumors about human women dying in childbirth again, I will make you pay. We have enough problems on this planet."

He narrows his eyes. "The fact the tribe queen survived is nothing more than luck. Do you think we can't see the size difference between Braxians and humans? You should thank me for preparing your friends for their fate."

Zoey shakes her head. "You know nothing about us, and instead of being embarrassed by your ignorance, you spread it like a disease. Human women have more strength in their vaginas than you have in your entire body, so you need to shut your fool mouth before I shut it for you."

I'm hard, I realize, as I stare at the scene in front of me. I wrestle with the urge to stride toward Zoey, fist her long hair, and slam my mouth down on hers. My father glowers at her, and I step forward. Enough.

Zoey sends me one burning look that warns me not to intervene, and I wave my hand, giving her space as my father lifts his lip in a sneer.

"What could your weak human body do to me?"

Zoey smiles. "You know how I killed the Dokhalls in that cave? Poison. Be very careful not to push me."

I stare at her. I know Zoey would never poison my father. But he doesn't know that.

"You dare threaten me?"

Her smile widens. "It's not a threat. It's a fucking promise. The women in this camp have enough to deal with without narrow-minded idiots spreading rumors."

My father reddens at that, but a tiny flash of respect sparks in his eyes as Zoey turns and stalks away.

It would be easier to stop breathing than it would be to not follow her. So I don't even try.

"Tagiz," my father hisses, but I pretend I can't hear him as I stride past him, keeping the furious female in my sight as she stomps between the kradis, muttering angrily to herself.

I stalk her, ignoring the way she glances over her shoulder at me, making it clear I'm not welcome anywhere near her.

"You made an enemy of my father, little healer."

Her jaw sticks out. "I don't care."

I laugh, and she glowers at me. But I'm not laughing at her. I'm laughing at the sheer ludicrousness of my actions up until this point.

I'm laughing in disbelief at the fact I thought I could ever give Zoey up.

I follow her to her kradi, and relief courses through my body. I no longer have a constant weight pressing on my chest. The decision has been made. Of course I couldn't stay away from my little healer. Of course I can't give her up. Asking me to do so is like asking the sun to no longer shine.

When Zoey was taken...my blood turned to ice. I couldn't imagine never seeing her again. All I wanted was to keep her safe in my kradi for the rest of our lives. The sight of the bruise on her cheek still makes me want to roar.

The way I feel about her...it's all instinct. I become feral at the thought of losing her—of watching her gift her smile to someone else for the rest of our lives. Or worse, never again seeing that smile light up her face.

Zoey turns once we reach her kradi. She stares at me, and I realize I must look insane as I throw my head back, still chuckling at the thought of falling in line with my father's plans and giving her up. I truly thought I could do it, and that's the most amusing thought of all. Because I would burn down this world for Zoey.

So now I have to prove myself to her.

I will lose my father over this, and my mother will likely stand beside him. His friends and their families will probably shun me. But if my father's love is only dependent on my doing what he wants, then it's not love at all.

Zoey's words run through my head.

"Maybe you feel like you need to live up to the idea of what Calix wants you to be simply because you feel like you owe him for taking you in as a child. But any decent person would've done the exact same thing."

They would have. If my father loved me, would he want me to never know the pleasure of a true mating?

If I choose to do what my father wants, I'm ruining four lives. Malis, Heric, Zoey—none of them want this mating. And for me, the thought of never touching Zoey's soft skin again, never kissing her soft lips, makes me want to roar.

Even worse, I allowed my father to poison my thoughts. I believed him when he said human females were weak. The idea is absurd. My little healer is tougher and smarter than most warriors.

I step closer, my hand finding Zoey's cheek. She closes her eyes, and I brush my thumb along her neck, watching as her skin breaks out in goose bumps.

"Your body knows you belong to me, little healer."

"Tagiz," Zoey says, but we're interrupted by Kroniz as he runs toward us.

"Dokhalls have been spotted near our territory," he says. "Rakiz wants a full defense."

I nod, my eyes still on Zoey's face.

"We will continue this later," I say. She shrugs, turning and walking into her kradi, and I grind my teeth in frustration.

First, I will make sure this camp is safe. Then I will win my little healer back to my side.

Zoey

"Zoey?"

I look up from my food. I'm eating lunch with a group of the new women, attempting to forget the weird look on Tagiz's face before he left to fight the Dokhalls.

I stare into the distance, my stomach tense. I chewed out Calix in front of his son, making an enemy of him. If I thought my situation was bad before, threatening to poison Tagiz's dad definitely didn't make it better.

I can't bring myself to apologize though. The look of terror in Nevada's eyes when Jozet blurted out she was going to die and Ellie's shaking hands...childbirth is scary enough. These babies are just the beginning for the human women here. And I won't have their pregnancies tainted by terror.

Still. I probably shouldn't have called Calix a narrow-minded idiot.

Even if he is one.

Now Tagiz is somewhere out there, fighting against the Dokhalls.

My stomach clenches, and I push away my plate at the thought. What if he gets hurt? Or worse?

"Zoey?"

I blink. I shouldn't have come to lunch when my mind is so clearly elsewhere.

"Sorry. I was just...thinking."

One of the women gives me a knowing look, her moss-green eyes narrowing on my face. Makayla, I think her name is.

"Thinking about Tagiz?"

I shrug. This camp isn't small enough for me to escape the sympathetic looks that are going to appear on everyone's faces when Tagiz mates with Malis, making it clear whatever obligation and guilt he feels toward his dad is bigger than anything he feels for me.

The atmosphere turns serious as Clara arrives, placing her plate down on the grass in front of her. We're sitting in the clearing where I talked with Ellie, and if we weren't watching Braxian kids attack each other with fake swords, we could be sitting in any park on Earth.

"Hey, ladies," Clara says, sitting down. She's tall and slim, with curly blonde hair and a light dusting of freckles scattered across her nose and cheeks. She looks delicate, but I recently saw her throw a Braxian warrior over her shoulder while she was training. Granted, the warrior was a teenager, but she planted her foot on his chest and lifted one eyebrow while he scowled up at her.

"So I've been thinking," Clara says, and Aria laughs.

"What else is new?" she murmurs, and I grin. Aria has long wine-colored hair that reminds me a little of Ivy's, but unlike the firefighter, Aria is pint-sized, with the creamy skin and delicate features of a porcelain doll. She's also hilarious, with a love of practical jokes.

"Anyway," Clara says, throwing Aria a look. The other woman gives her an easy grin but pretends to zip her lips. "When the Dokhalls separated into smaller groups, they became more of a threat, not less. It allowed them to be sneaky and move around in a way they couldn't as a large group. Just look at what they did to Zoey and Nevada."

The other women glance at me, and I fight not to squirm.

"I agree," I say. "The Dokhalls have no true loyalty to each other. If a group of them can get that ship, they'll leave the rest of their people here in a heartbeat."

Clara nods. "So if we want to take them all out at once, we need to be able to get them all to show up at the same place at the same time."

"Makes sense," I say. "But the Dokhalls are brutal and smart." I brush my hand over the bruise on my cheek and fight to ignore the way my ribs seem to twinge at the reminder of just how brutal they are. "We'd have to lay the kind of trap they can't ignore."

Clara blows out a breath, and we all go silent. She nods her head once, straightening her shoulders. "I think we need to tell them we'll give them the ship."

Everyone explodes, talking at once. Clara raises her hand, and I have to admire the way she takes back control.

"We let it leak we're tired of being targeted and we want to stay here. After Zoey and Nevada were kidnapped, we've realized the Dokhalls are too dangerous. We're willing to give them the ship if they leave and swear never to come back."

"Why would they believe us?" Makayla asks.

"We tell them we're staying with the Braxians. We don't trust that the ship will work if we take it. Plus, we don't have the chip anyway."

I chew on my lip. "It's risky. If we lure them close to the ship, we have to take most of them out. If they survive, they'll be gunning for us. Not to mention, the ship was already damaged in the last battle. What if it gets damaged again?"

"And what if they have the chip?" Eloise pipes up. "All they'd have to do is get on the ship and they can take it."

"We have part of their thruster," Aria says.

A woman I haven't been introduced to snorts. "I bet they'll take the risk anyway. We don't know how far their planet is from Agron. If its close, they might be able to make it even if the ship is damaged."

Clara angles her head, her eyes serious. "There are risks," she says. "And if you guys can think of another way to lure all the Dokhalls into the same area at the same time, I'm willing to hear it. But I think this is the only way."

"If we do this, we have to find a way to take them all out at once," Aria says.

"What about the explosives you guys used last time?" Eloise asks. "The pods?"

I shake my head. "If we're luring the Dokhalls close to the ship, the pods are a bad idea. The last thing we need is to blow a hole in the side of the ship by mistake."

The beginning of an idea is simmering in my head. It's the kind of idea that if I execute it, it'll change me. Forever.

"I have a few thoughts," I say. "But first, we need to see if luring the Dokhalls to the ship is even possible and if we have the numbers we'd need to take them down. Let me talk to Nevada and Rakiz."

Tonight, the entire camp will be celebrating the arrival of their baby girl. Danica represents hope to a tribe that rarely sees female babies. Alexis convinced Dragix to move the old ship that was leaking fuel into the Braxians' drinking water, and while she's hoping it will help with the uneven male-to-female birth ratio, it's still far too soon to tell.

"Zoey! Oh, thank God!"

I jump to my feet as Ellie rushes into the clearing. "What is it? Is it the baby?"

"No," she says. "It's Hewex."

CHAPTER FIFTEEN

Z oey

I sprint to the healers' kradi, finding a group of warriors gathered outside. I elbow my way through them, and a familiar voice roars at them to let me past.

Tagiz reaches for my elbow, hauling me through the crowd.

"How bad is it?" I ask.

His gaze darts away, and my heart sinks.

"Oh God."

From the moment I was rescued, Hewex has been a staple in my life. Sure, he's grumpy and impatient, but he's also kind. When I was recovering in the healers' kradi, he would bring me snacks and tell me all about Agron, encouraging me to get better so I could see it myself.

I choke out a sob when I reach Hewex. He's lying on one of the beds, and Tagiz steps up next to him. Moni is attempting to push his intestines back into his body.

They gutted him.

I step closer to Moni. "Can I help?" I murmur.

She nods. "I can't see any perforated organs, but I must stop the bleeding. Hand me those clean rags."

I wash my hands quickly and then grab them, using them to pack the wound myself.

The pain must be intolerable, but Hewex pushes away the tonic one of the other healers offers him.

"Need...to...tell...you."

Tagiz's expression is terrible. The two men have been partners for years, working together. Tagiz once told me Hewex taught him everything he knows. That he thinks of him as an older brother.

Tagiz leans over. "Quickly, then. Get it out and take the tonic. You shouldn't be awake for this."

"Some of their light-sticks still work perfectly," Hewex gasps out. "They took our group by surprise. We were over-confident after fighting the Dokhalls that attacked when Nevada and Zoey were taken. Their light-sticks paralyzed us." His jaw tightens, and he looks away. "They killed all the warriors but me. I am to be a warning. Cooperate or die."

Bile rises, and it feels like I can't take a full breath. It's never going to be over. They're going to keep planning, keep attacking until we give them what they want.

Hewex finally takes the pain tonic, and Moni finishes stitching him up. We're all quiet as we watch.

I hang around for a while, making sure Moni doesn't need anything else. But she and the other healers seem to have it under control. Even though the Braxians recover from injuries quickly, I wouldn't wish the kind of recovery Hewex will have on anyone. Not without drugs.

Drugs.

I glance at Moni. "I'm going to go collect a few things."

Moni nods, her eyes on Hewex. "Bring back more ortar leaves, please."

Tagiz's eyes meet mine. "Do you want me to come with you?"

I shake my head. "Stay with Hewex."

His gaze searches my face, his jaw tightening at whatever he sees, but he finally nods.

I collect Jozet on the way, and a few minutes later, I'm inhaling the sweet smell of greenery. I'm instantly calmer.

Jozet is watching me closely. He seems to realize I need space though, and he's staying at least ten feet away so I have the illusion of privacy.

I'm tired.

Every time I close my eyes, all I can see are the bars of that cage. All I can hear are the taunts of the Voildi as they discussed whether or not I'd live long enough to be able to be sold.

Occasionally in my dreams, I'm standing on that stage on that strange planet, the Dokhalls bidding on me. And then, not long after, I trip and fall, and all I can hear is the crack of my ribs as one of them kicks me while I'm down.

But now I have a new dream. Nevada, her face pale, jaw tight as she glares at the Dokhalls. I can't stop thinking about the blind determination on her face as she tried to bargain with me to take her baby and run. And the way the Dokhalls took us right from under the Braxians' noses.

I'm pretty sure I know what I'll see in my dreams tonight.

Hewex, lying helpless on the ground as the Dokhalls taunt him, cutting him up. His friends dead.

Because of us.

Don't get me wrong. I don't blame myself or the other human women. We were taken from our homes, and we've been doing whatever it takes to survive. Thanks to the Braxians, we're all doing much better than we could've expected.

But the Braxians were just living their lives before we came along. Since then, they've been focused on protecting us, keeping us safe. Fighting in battles and wars and constantly pivoting to face new threats.

The other women are right. Something has to be done.

I know I don't look well. Jozet frowned at me a few minutes ago, and Moni constantly remarks on my dark circles. She offered me a sleeping tonic again, but I'm terrified of being stuck in the dreams, unable to wake up. The best sleep I've had on Agron was the one I had in Tagiz's arms.

But there's only one thing that will truly make me feel safe again.

The death of all the remaining Dokhalls.

I search the forest floor until I find the tiny yellow mushrooms I've been looking for. I stare at them, hesitating.

The words I intoned at my graduation spring to mind.

I solemnly pledge...

I lean forward and pluck three of the mushrooms, my breath coming in short pants.

...to practice my profession faithfully.

On to the moss. I find the specific kind I need crawling up one of the white tree trunks scattered here and there within the forest. It needs to be old, and I gesture for Jozet to lean up high and help me scrape some of the darker moss near one of the thicker branches.

That also goes into my basket.

I will abstain from whatever is deleterious and mischievous...

My hands tremble slightly, but I firm them. The next ingredient takes longer to find. Long enough that I wonder if Jozet is getting impatient, but when I glance over my shoulder, he's leaning against a tree, sharpening one of his knives.

The flower is a bright orange. But it's the roots that I need, and I carefully dig around the plant until I can cut out a small section.

...and will not take or knowingly administer any harmful drug...

I stride to the clearing where I spotted the white flowers I hadn't seen before, last time I was in this part of the forest with Sarissa and Nevada. Now I know what they are.

I will do all in my power to maintain and elevate the standard of my profession...

It's my lips that tremble this time, but I firm them as I pluck a few of the petals.

...and will hold in confidence all personal matters committed to my keeping.

One last ingredient. This plant looks similar to belladonna on Earth, also known as deadly nightshade.

It's perfectly innocent when used alone. It's not until it's combined with the other ingredients in my basket that it will have the intended effect.

On Earth, I dedicated my life to healing. I took my pledge seriously.

I will devote myself to the welfare of those committed to my care.

I blink back the tears that threaten to rise as I snatch a few of the leaves and get back to my feet. This, combined with the maradoza berries, will give me everything I need.

I'm no longer on Earth. And I won't let the Dokhalls take anything else from me.

A part of me, the small, innocent part of me that's standing on stage with her friends, reciting the pledge...that part shrivels up and dies.

It's replaced with a savage woman who will do whatever it takes to survive. Even if it means betraying everything I thought I stood for.

Tagiz

I grind my teeth, frustration coursing through my body. I was forced to leave Hewex's side for another meeting with my father. Moni says the warrior will likely live, but even when he is back on his feet, he will deal with the pain for some time.

And instead of supporting the friend who has been at my side all this time, I am once again listening to my father rant about duty.

I glance at Malis, and her face is pale and drawn. She looks like a shadow of her former self, and I am beginning to feel the same. Our parents' expectations are sucking the life and vitality from us.

Enough.

My father is ranting, two gold bands in his hand. Apparently, Malis's father found them beneath Malis's pillow. Heric is growing impatient.

"Father," I interrupt, and he ceases his pacing, turning to scowl at me. Malis's father is lounging on a chair across the kradi, his eyes dark.

"By now, you know Malis and I have no intention of mating," I say. I glance at Malis, and her mouth drops open, hope shining in her eyes.

"Don't be ridiculous," my father snaps, and I sigh.

"I will mate Zoey," I say, getting to my feet. His mouth drops open as my mother gasps.

"Tagiz," she murmurs, and I shake my head.

"This plan of yours is causing so much pain," I say. "Can you not see that? Malis and I are never going to want to be mated. Would you truly want us to be miserable together?"

My father stares at me, and a muscle jumps in his jaw. "You have always known this is the expectation we have for you. And now you choose to throw away all our plans for a *human?*"

I narrow my eyes at him. "Be careful," I warn him. "I will not tolerate you speaking about her with disrespect."

He hisses in disbelief. "After everything we have done for you, you would throw it back in our faces? You were nobody—just another orphan when we took you in. We made you a warrior."

I stare at him. Guilt rips through me, but I push it down. Zoey is worth my father's anger. She is worth everything.

"*I* made myself a warrior. You gave me opportunities I am thankful for. But it was *I* who trained for hours every day. It was *I* who left this camp constantly to hunt and fight. Would you truly have me beholden to you for the rest of my life?"

"You would dishonor me this way? Dishonor Malis?"

Malis shakes her head, finding the voice that has been continually silenced since we were told we would be mates.

"There is no dishonor when it comes to choosing love," she says.

"Love?" my father spits. Behind him, Malis's father is getting to his feet, his face burning with cold rage.

"Yes," Malis says through trembling lips. "I love Heric, and Tagiz loves Zoey. Why would you have us ruin our lives this way?"

"It's not about *you*," Malis's father snaps. "This mating is about producing the strongest bloodlines to continue to stay close to the tribe king."

"I am already close to the tribe king," I say. "And I can tell you with full certainty, if Rakiz truly knew the plans you had in place and why, no one in either of our families would ever be trusted to be so close to power again."

"You may be close to the tribe king, but what about my daughter?"

Malis's lip quivers. "Father—"

My father holds up a hand. "This is ludicrous. We have waited long enough."

I laugh. "What you want to happen is not happening. I suggest you move on." I survey my father, blocking out everyone else. "I will always be grateful for your actions that day. You could have killed me, true, although I don't believe your honor would have allowed you to. But I will not enter a loveless mating simply to keep you happy. And neither will Malis."

My father is turning a dull purple, and my mother is staring at me as if she no longer recognizes me. My heart clenches. I knew I would lose my father, but I hoped...

I will still not change my mind.

"Do you know what Zoey said to me when she saw me with Malis recently?" I ask, and my father sneers.

"Do not speak that name in my kradi."

I ignore him. Her words have echoed over and over in my head since the day she spoke them, and I have them memorized.

"I just want you to be happy," I say, keeping my eyes on my father's face. "Do whatever it is that makes you feel good, Tagiz. Live the life you want, and that will be enough for me." I laugh bitterly. "Do you know what that is, father? That's called *unconditional love*. Wanting someone to be happy more than you want them to be yours. Wanting someone to *feel good* even if it means they don't do it by your side. Real love doesn't come with threats and deals. It doesn't mean you're obligated to live your life a certain way so you can deserve that love."

"You think to lecture *me?*"

I shrug. "I believe you must not have ever known real love if this is what you think it is. And if this is true, I am sorry for that. But we are leaving."

I take Malis's hand in mine, ignoring the way her parents bluster, and my eyes meet my mother's one last time. She's pale, her lips trembling, but she gives me a tiny nod.

Malis wipes her face, raising her head high. And then we both walk out of my father's kradi and toward the ones we love.

CHAPTER SIXTEEN

T agiz

In spite of the attack, Rakiz looks happier than I've ever seen him. Earlier, he visited Hewex, who insisted this celebration still go ahead.

"He said to grab happiness by both hands whenever it appears," Rakiz told me. "So that is what I'm doing." He slapped me on the shoulder. "I suggest you do the same."

His nose is still swollen from its encounter with my fist, and my cheek is bruised and scabbing.

But now he sits next to Nevada at the head of his table, one of his fingers stroking his daughter's tiny cheek as he murmurs in his mate's ear. Nevada laughs at whatever he says, taking the baby from him as she begins to fuss.

The entire camp has come out to celebrate the birth of the tribe king's daughter. I take a moment to scan the clearing, noting how much larger our tribe seems now, with the new human women along with the temporary addition of Dexar and some of his warriors.

The qatai stalks over to Rakiz, slapping him on the back as he gazes down at Danica. He turns his attention to Alexis, a look of promise in his eyes, and she grins back at him, raising her eyebrows suggestively.

Someone begins playing music, and Beth reaches for Zarix, who sways with her in the center of the clearing. A few more couples join them, and I nod at my father as he holds court at his table.

"Do you think the human females will be able to use the spaceship?" Jozet asks.

I turn to him, and he hands me a cup. His gaze is on one of the new human females, and his eyes light with challenge as she meets his gaze and quickly glances away.

"Tagiz, Jozet," Nevada calls.

Jozet's cheeks turn red as we move closer to our tribe queen. He almost squirms as Nevada raises her eyebrow at him.

"I apologize for my words in the cave," he says, and she snorts.

"You're not the first male to panic during labor, and you won't be the last. You kept us safe, and that's all I needed." She pulls the cloth away from the bundle in her arms. "You can hold her if you want."

Jozet immediately puts his hands behind his back, shaking his head, and Nevada laughs.

"Tagiz?"

I clear my throat, taking the baby, conscious of Rakiz watching me closely. She's light. So light she barely weighs anything at all. But the babe is beautiful, her tiny hand clutching my finger.

Zoey approaches, grinning at Nevada. "You look happy." She leans around my arm, cooing at Danica, who studies her face.

"You look beautiful," I murmur to Zoey. Her dress is new, and the blue perfectly matches her eyes. Her hair is piled on her head, long strands falling in places as if she has just been tumbled.

She smiles at me, but it doesn't meet her eyes, and she quickly glances away. I offer her the baby, and she doesn't hesitate, cuddling the tiny bundle close as she sways to the music. She sniffs at Danica's head. "God, that baby smell is like a drug," she murmurs, and Nevada laughs.

"You're a natural with her," she says, and Zoey smiles, still swaying as she gazes down at Danica.

I'm hit with a bolt of primal lust. A need to ensure when Zoey clutches her own babe to her, that babe is *mine*. Rakiz meets my gaze, a half smile on his face as if he can read my thoughts.

Zoey's eyes meet mine over the baby's head, and I barely refrain from taking her mouth, from claiming her in front of my entire tribe. There are too many eyes on us right now, however, and I have far too much to say.

She glances away, her shoulders stiff, and I want to pull her aside, to make her listen to me. But I will wait until she is ready.

Charlie approaches, looking lost without Dragix by her side.

"How are you doing?" Nevada asks her, patting the seat next to her.

Charlie leans over and places a kiss on the top of Danica's head before slumping into a chair. "Dragix is due back tomorrow. About damn time. I swear, being separated from him is the worst."

Zoey grins. "Well, that's not surprising. You guys were practically joined at the hip before he let you come back here."

Charlie nods. "Have you guys heard anything from Vivian and Sarissa yet?"

"Nope. The other women seem to be pinning all their hopes on them though. No pressure." Nevada laughs.

"Speaking of...I need to talk to you guys tomorrow," Zoey murmurs to Nevada, and the tribe queen raises her eyebrow.

"We can talk about it now."

"It's okay. You should enjoy this night before we talk about revenge plans."

Nevada claps her hands. "My favorite thing. Gimme."

Zoey laughs, slowly lowering herself into the chair next to Charlie, and I realize the baby has fallen asleep in her arms. Tenderness unfurls in my chest at the sight, and I claim the chair next to her.

Zoey ignores me, but I am content to simply be in her presence.

"I've created something that might help against the Dokhalls," she says.

"What kind of something?" Nevada asks. Next to her, Rakiz leans forward, obviously interested in this conversation as well.

"A poison. One that should level the playing field, considering they still have those light-sticks."

Nevada raises her eyebrows, and my hand itches with the need to take Zoey's hand in mine. From the look on her face, my gentle little healer is already upset at the thought of taking more Dokhall lives.

"What kind of poison?"

Zoey shrugs. "The deadly kind. I'm not sure the best way

to use it right now, which is why I wanted to talk to you guys about it. It could be used to poison their drinking source, or we could dip arrowheads into it if we're luring the Dokhalls to the ship. We may even be able to use it in the air if we can get them somewhere inside. I'm not entirely sure."

Rakiz nods. "This is good news. We need every weapon we can get in this fight. Thank you, Zoey."

My little healer nods, a slight blush rising on her cheeks, but she has become pale.

I lean over, murmuring into her ear. "I need to talk to you."

Her gaze jumps to mine and then shifts across the clearing to where my father is watching us.

I move until my body is blocking her view of my father. "I need to speak with you privately," I murmur.

She glances back toward my parents. Her chin juts out, and I almost bury my hand in her hair and lay her on the table in front of everyone. Nothing makes me harder than watching my little healer be stubborn.

"That's not a good idea," Zoey says.

"Leave my father for me to handle, little healer."

She shakes her head. "I don't think you understand, Tagiz. I'm done with this."

She gently passes the baby back to Nevada and walks away, taking my heart with her.

Zoey

I spend the next day in the healers' kradi, where I see a few patients under Moni's watchful eye. Two warriors are injured after skirmishes at the border of Rakiz's territory. A small group of Dokhalls attacked with no warning. Fortunately, their light-sticks weren't working, and they obviously underestimated how well trained Rakiz's warriors are. They won't be attacking any more Braxians.

My heart hurts for Hewex's friends who are currently being buried. Rakiz's face was hard when he stalked into the healers' kradi earlier, talking briefly with Hewex. The warrior gained consciousness long enough to murmur briefly to the tribe king, and then Moni shooed Rakiz away, ordering Hewex to drink more of her tonic.

I examine one of the warrior's shoulders before cleaning and then covering the wound with the antiseptic paste Moni prefers.

"Does that feel better?"

He nods. "Thank you."

It felt good to tell Nevada and Rakiz about the poison I've created. I no longer feel like a victim. I'm fighting back, and I'm doing it in my own way.

I'll never be on the front lines of a battle, and I don't want to be. I'm content saving lives in the healers' kradi. But after what the Dokhalls have done to us, I need to play a part in their downfall.

Rakiz has agreed to give me my own kradi where I can mix my poisons. He said he'll have a guard stationed nearby to make sure no one gets too curious. And Moni has said she will use her own knowledge to help me tweak what I've already created. She didn't seem surprised when I told her what I was working on. She simply told me once again that some of the deadliest plants grow in the Seinex Forest.

The afternoon passes quickly, and I focus on mixing up new tonics and salves, checking on Hewex, and keeping myself busy.

Yes, I'm burying myself in work. And yes, part of the

reason I'm doing that is because I'm worried if I don't, I'll end up finding Tagiz, falling to my knees, and begging him to choose *me*.

Life is no longer in color. It's now black and white and gray and *sad*. And I don't know what to do about it.

I'm so deep in thought it's not until Ivy and Charlie are standing right in front of me that I realize they've been trying to get my attention.

"Sorry." I blush. "I'm walking around like I'm sleep-walking."

"It's okay," Ivy murmurs. "You want to talk about it?"

"Maybe later. What are you guys up to?"

"We've been hanging with Makayla and Clara. You know, they're pretty damn excited about your poison. That's badass, Zoey." Ivy glances around the healers' kradi curiously, and I smile.

"We have to see if it'll work before we get too excited."

Charlie nudges me with her elbow. "If it doesn't, you'll find something else. But poison is a good way to go. The Dokhalls are armed with those stupid stick things. And even if they don't work all the time, they work just enough of the time to give them a huge advantage."

I nod, my mind going to Hewex. He's doing better today, but it'll likely be a while before he can be on his feet. "You're right. I just...I really want to make sure we can get everyone who wants to leave on that ship, you know?"

Charlie tilts her head. "Yeah, I get it. I want that too. But I also know sometimes you think the grass is greener somewhere else. And then you realize it's not grass at all. It's that fake shit they roll out to hide the dry dirt underneath."

I grin at that. "You have a point. I like the grass here just fine. But the other women haven't been here anywhere near as long as we have. Remember when we first landed? All we wanted was to get home."

Ivy nods. "Not only that, but it sounds like they had it worse on the spaceship too. Apparently one of the women was killed. I don't blame them for wanting revenge. I just wonder how likely it is they'll be able to get it."

I wash my hands and hang up my apron, waving goodbye to Moni, who is examining Hewex on the other side of the kradi.

The sun is high in the sky as I make my way to the training arena with Charlie and Ivy gossiping the whole time.

Ivy lets out a wolf whistle as we approach the arena, and I can't help but laugh. Vrex is currently fighting Terex. Both of them have their shirts off, swinging their swords. Vrex says something to make Terex laugh, and Ivy sighs, her eyes softening as she gazes at Vrex. "That man. This morning he brought me breakfast in bed. He feels guilty that we're not hanging out at our hut in the woods."

The sun disappears, and we all look up. "Dragix is coming in hot," Ivy murmurs.

"Is that Tagiz on his back?" Charlie asks.

The dragon roars, and I slam my hands over my ears. "What the hell?"

He lands no further than ten feet from us, with a thump that shakes the ground as he roars again.

I meet Tagiz's eyes, and he leaps from Dragix's back, rolling clear of the obviously furious dragon.

"Who pissed in his Cheerios?" Ivy snaps.

Dragix *moves,* and Ivy and I jump back as he reaches out one foot and pulls Charlie close to him. Her eyes widen in surprise, and he drops his head to her stomach. We're all silent as he inhales through his nose.

Rakiz approaches, and Dragix angles his head, blowing out a stream of fire in warning. Rakiz scowls at him, freezing in place, his hand on his sword.

"Dragix," Charlie murmurs. Then she raises her eyebrows. "You can seriously smell that?" The dragon keeps his eyes on her stomach, and I get it.

"Oooh." I grin.

Charlie glances at us, her cheeks heating. "Yes. Someone just discovered he's going to be a daddy."

Ivy's mouth drops open as she glances at me. Charlie begins talking to Dragix softly, urging him to shift. Another growl sounds, and I almost throw up my hands at the drama of it all.

But that last growl didn't come from Dragix.

My furry little beast has jumped in front of me, and he's currently baring his teeth at Dragix as if daring the dragon to attack.

"I thought we agreed you'd stay in the kradi." I sigh. Ivy tilts her head at me like she can't believe what she's hearing, and on the other side of the training arena, Tagiz steps up next to Rakiz, both their gazes narrowed on my karja.

Uh-oh.

Dragix's head swivels around Charlie's back, and one gold eye stares at the karja.

The fur ball stares back, teeth still bared as a low growl sounds from its throat.

"I bet it's a male," Ivy murmurs. "Just wait. One of them is about to piss in a circle and mark its territory."

I shrug. "It is a male. His name is Harry."

She gives me a look that suggests I might be completely insane.

"Right. Because what wild animal on an alien planet wouldn't be called Harry?"

"I always wanted a dog," I say defensively. "And I wanted to name him Harry. Besides, he likes his name. Don't you, darling?"

Harry swings his head, giving me a growl that sounds a lot like affirmation in my head.

"Who are you, and what have you done with Zoey?"

I shrug. "Come on, Harry. You're a big, bad, brave boy, but even you are no match for a dragon."

The karja ignores me, still focused on Dragix. Dragix shifts into a man, and it drives the karja wild. He loses his mind, growling at the dragon as if challenging him to a fight.

Dragix stares at Harry for a few seconds, and the karja loses whatever dominance contest he thought he could win. Just like that, he drops to his belly, angling his head submissively.

Dragix turns his attention back to Charlie. On the other side of the training arena, Rakiz is ordering his men away from the dragon.

Dragix stares intently at Charlie, and I can tell they're having one of their spooky silent conversations. She frowns at him, and he nods, his hand stroking over her flat belly.

He turns to Rakiz. "I apologize. The scent of our babe slammed into me, and all I could see was that Charlie was surrounded by warriors."

Rakiz nods. "I understand," he says. "This is a...difficult time for males."

My mouth drops open. Ivy snorts, and Charlie angles her head. "I'm sorry," she says sweetly. "I must have misheard you. Did you just say this is a difficult time for *males?*"

I grin. Charlie has a temper. A temper Dragix loves, if the look on his face is any indication.

"You are more vulnerable when you are carrying a child," he says carefully. "It is...instinct to protect you."

"Uh-huh. I can no longer smell meat cooking without wanting to puke. But please, tell me more about how difficult it is for *you*."

Dragix grins at her, then swings her up into his arms. He's obviously delighted at the news, and after hearing about his history with the Braxians, I can understand why he lost his mind for a brief moment.

Thankfully, he seems to have regained control because he carries Charlie toward the kradis, his naked butt flexing with each step.

"Wow," Ivy says as we watch him leave.

I sigh. "I know, right?"

"Ivy," a low voice rumbles, and we both jump as Vrex appears. He looks unimpressed with Ivy's admiration of Dragix's toned ass, and she squeals as he throws her over his shoulder before also marching toward his own kradi as she howls with laughter.

"Zoey." I jump again as Tagiz appears out of nowhere.

"Jeez, give a girl some warning," I mutter, still staring after Charlie and Ivy, jealousy twisting its claws into my heart.

"That could be us," he says, following my gaze.

I open my mouth, unsure what, exactly, I'll say, and Tagiz buries his hand in my hair.

His kiss is possessive. It's a claiming, and he's clearly marking his territory for all to see. I frown, about to give him a piece of my mind, but his lips gentle, caressing mine, and I soften against him.

He pulls away. "I am giving you space, little healer. But soon, I will grow tired of allowing you to run from me. Soon, I will make you listen to what I have to say."

I narrow my eyes at him, still wanting to know how he snuck away from camp without me noticing and where the hell he went with Dragix.

But he turns and stalks away.

CHAPTER SEVENTEEN

T agiz

It's early in the morning, the sun barely risen in the sky. The breeze is cool, the sun is warm, and my blood is hot.

Zoey is training with Kroniz. I don't know how this happened, but I suspect Hewex is responsible. I have heard her begging him to teach her to fight, and my hands fist at the fact she never asked me.

Why would she ask me? She believes I thought her weak. I *did* think her weaker than a Braxian female, but over the past days, Zoey has shown me the error of those thoughts.

Kroniz says something to make her laugh as he hands her one of the practice swords.

She throws her head back, revealing the smooth pale skin at her throat, and my eye twitches.

He grins at her, and my teeth grind together.

He gestures for her to move closer to him, and my hand reaches for my sword.

My hand tightens around the hilt of that sword as Kroniz steps even closer to Zoey, showing her how to dodge away as he swings his own practice sword. It should be me teaching her to defend herself. Me standing between her and anyone who would think to hurt her for the rest of our lives.

I want to roar with fury as I watch them finish their training. Hewex owes me an explanation for this.

He knows how I feel about the little healer.

I have to leave before I do something I regret, and I storm toward the healers' kradi, infuriated.

Hewex is awake, although his eyes are glassy.

"You put Kroniz in charge of Zoey's combat training," I growl.

He shrugs, wincing with the movement, and the sight of his pain takes the edge off my fury. Barely.

"He owed me a favor."

I bare my teeth at him, and he gives me a mild look in return.

"You will soon be a mated male, from what I hear," he says. "Zoey has been training with Kroniz for many mornings. You have simply been unaware."

"We're almost brothers. And you betray me like this?"

He rolls his eyes—something I've never seen him do before—and it's clear he's been spending time with Zoey. The thought makes my hands shake.

"You should get used to the thought of her with others. Although, you're unlikely to have to see it."

I don't bother correcting Hewex. I haven't yet told him I have made it clear to my father I won't be mating with Malis.

"What do you mean?"

He frowns up at the ceiling of the kradi. "I overheard

Moni talking to one of the other healers. Zoey is training one of the younger females to take her place here." He gestures around him at the healers' kradi. "She has decided when the ship is fixed, she will be leaving Agron."

My heart pounds in my chest, and my fists clench, my hands empty when they should be filled with my little healer.

"What are you talking about?"

Moni approaches, a cup in her hand. "Enough," she murmurs. "Hewex must rest if he is to heal."

His eyes are already sliding closed, and I barely tamp down the urge to shake him, to demand he tell me more.

I feel as if I'm floating above my body as I stumble out of the healers' kradi.

And almost walk into my mother.

My mouth drops open as I reach out a hand to steady her. She blinks up at me.

"I thought you might be here," she murmurs. "I've been looking for you."

"Are you here to formally disown me?" My voice is gruff, and I wish I could take back the words as she flinches.

"I-I can see why you might think that, Tagiz. But no. I would like to talk to you."

Part of me wants to refuse her. "Did Father send you to convince me to change my mind about mating with Malis?"

"No. He doesn't know I'm here."

I frown at that, and she gives me a tiny, hopeful smile. "Please, Tagiz."

I glance around, noting the curious eyes on us. I don't want to take her back to my kradi, as it's too close to my parents' kradi. Besides, it's full of memories of Zoey. The kind of memories I have no desire to share with my mother.

If I can even call her my mother anymore.

Her hands are shaking, and I sigh. "I know a quiet place."

I take her to the stream, my favorite spot, where I stood with Zoey. It feels like years have passed since that day, and I frown at the water before gesturing for my mother to sit down on a large, flat rock.

Her eyes turn dreamy as she stares into the water, and for a moment, the only sounds come from the wind whistling through the trees and the water bubbling over smooth stones.

"What is it you want, Mother?"

She turns her head, and I tense as her eyes gleam with tears.

"I should have been a better mother to you," she murmurs.

I frown. "What do you mean?"

"I have failed as a mother. It was my job to protect you, to make you feel safe. Instead, I made you feel as if you had to earn our love."

"Father made it clear what my tasks would be when he said he would take me as his own."

She shakes her head, and a tear rolls down her cheek. "Your father never told you the truth. It was I who saw you that day. I peeked into the kradi where he had put you, and I saw you sitting there, so lonely. You were too small, too thin, yet your shoulders were back, your head was raised. I knew then you would be a fierce warrior. But more importantly, I knew you were mine."

"You—"

She nods. "By then, your father was close to giving up on having a child. He was furious with me."

I grind my teeth at that, thinking of Zoey's words. "It may

have been his body that did not allow you to have a child," I say, and her mouth falls open.

"How—never mind."

I sigh. "So why did he offer me the deal?"

She turns her head, brushing another tear off her face as she stares into the water as if it holds all the answers of the universe.

"I was best friends with the tribe queen," she murmurs. "Even then, forced matings were not allowed. My parents called our mating an 'arrangement,' but it was made clear your father and I would obey or we would be branded as dishonorable."

I grind my teeth. "And the tribe king knew?"

"No. But his mate did. When I told her I was unhappy in my mating and why, she was furious." She smiles. "She told me if I wanted to leave, if I wanted to move to another tribe, I would have her full support."

My mouth drops open at that. The idea is unthinkable. Father would have been a laughingstock.

"What does this have to do with me?"

"When I saw you, I didn't see a warrior. I didn't see a way to be close to the tribe king or queen. I saw my son. I saw the boy I would raise as my own. And I told your father. I told him you were our son, and if he didn't take you as ours, I would accept the tribe queen's offer."

Warmth begins to unfurl in my chest. "He must have been livid."

She nods. "He was. But he had also seen how you fought. He admired your bravery and skill with a sword, even then. He told me we would take you in, and you would be raised as our son under certain conditions."

"I would train until I was in Rakiz's inner circle and mate with the female he chose."

"Yes."

I scowl, turning away, but my mother's hand on my arm stills my movement.

I frown down at her. "Why are you telling me this?"

"Because you are *my son*," she whispers. "You were mine from the moment I saw you. I love you more than I could have ever imagined. And when I heard you defending your love for your female, I realized how badly I have hurt you with my actions." She lets out a sob, and I can't help it; I pull her into my arms. It's been so long since I hugged my mother that I forgot how small she is. She feels fine-boned and fragile, and the thought makes panic burn at the base of my neck.

"Mother—"

"I need you to know, Tagiz. I love you so fiercely that sometimes at night, I would stare up at the roof of our kradi and think of all the ways I could lose you. I would dream your real father was still alive and he was coming to take you away from me and I would have to pretend to be happy for you. Every time you left on a hunt, I would lie in my furs for days, just begging the gods to bring you back to me. I went along with your father's plans because that was our deal. He got a son who would fall in line with his plans, and I got *you.*"

I stare at her, stunned. All this time, I thought both my parents considered me nothing more than a tool they could use to keep them close and in favor with the qatai.

"I...love you too, Mother."

She buries her head against my chest and sobs. I hold her to me, gazing at the water. I'm even more furious at my father for the way he has treated my mother. But some small, broken part of me has begun to heal. One of my parents loves me. So much she is currently breaking apart as she wets my shirt with her tears.

"It's okay," I murmur. It takes a while before she can raise her head, wiping her damp face. "I forgive you," I say, and her eyes fill with tears again.

I laugh. "No more tears, Mother. Whatever happens between me and Calix has nothing to do with us, understood?"

Her eyes widen slightly as I use my father's name. But as far as I'm concerned, he's no longer my father until he apologizes to Zoey and begs my mother for forgiveness for the way he has treated her.

"Where is Zoey, Tagiz?"

I sigh, and it all comes pouring out of me. How she will no longer speak to me, will barely look at me. How I ruined the best thing to ever happen to me.

My mother listens and then smiles. "I never told you, but I was in love with another warrior when I mated with your father."

My mouth drops open. "What?"

She nods, and her face is sad, although her eyes have finally dried. "He was the love of my life, and on the day I mated with Calix, he left the tribe for good. I tell you this because I want you to know I understand what it feels like to love someone as you love Zoey. And I know she loves you too. It may feel like all hope is lost, but true love...it never dies."

I stare at her, still wrestling with this new information, and she gives me a smile that lights up her face.

"Go and win your female, my love. I can't wait to properly meet her."

CHAPTER EIGHTEEN

Z oey

I shiver as I collect the things I need in the forest. Jozet is on guard, but ever since the attack, this forest is teeming with Braxian warriors.

I thought I was doing better. But I barely slept last night. Each time I closed my eyes, it was like I was back on that slave planet. The crack of my ribs sounded again and again in my ears. Then the dreams shifted until I was watching Tagiz wrap mating bands around Malis's wrists, and all I wanted to do was run until I couldn't run anymore.

Finally, I gave up on sleep.

Most of the Braxian warriors simply nod at me when I appear to collect the ingredients Moni asks for. Rakiz has them constantly changing up where they're stationed, but there have been no more sightings of Dokhalls in the area.

I have no doubt they're planning something.

Just like us, they probably want to get home to their

planet. Home to their families. I feel a moment of nausea as the Dokhalls I killed flash in front of my eyes, and I stumble. I glance over my shoulder, but Jozet is sharpening his sword, his mind obviously elsewhere.

No, Zoey. Those Dokhalls bought you. They treated you like a product and almost killed you.

Logically, I know I did what anyone would have done in the same situation. I had a pregnant woman to protect, and if the Dokhalls woke up, they likely would have killed me.

But it doesn't change the fact I took three lives.

I bite down on my lower lip until it almost bleeds, glancing over my shoulder at Jozet.

The last few times I brought Jozet to the forest with me, he was practically vibrating with tension, ready for an attack. But now we tend to run into so many other guards in this area that he's gradually relaxed. Thank God because the more tense he is, the more nervous I get.

I've been visiting Nevada most days and cuddling her gorgeous little daughter. She has the tiniest toes and the shadow of green-blue scales across her chubby baby shoulders.

I wonder if mine and Tagiz's babies would have the same scales.

No, Zoey, we don't think about him anymore.

He still hasn't told me what he was doing with Dragix. He seems to be giving me space, although I constantly find him watching me, promise in his eyes. He doesn't go near Malis, who has been walking through camp with her own Braxian male by her side.

But I still don't trust it.

Mom once told me about how my father used to swear he would leave his wife. As soon as she got the courage to break things off with him, he would tell her he just needed a little more time. He kept her hanging on for years.

I don't think Tagiz is anything like my father. But he's an honorable man who feels beholden to Calix. And I can't compete with Braxian honor.

Jozet opens his mouth when I approach, my basket full. Inside the basket is a tiny wooden box, painstakingly carved. Beneath the smooth lid, the box has been divided into sections, allowing me to keep herbs and plants separated.

I found it beneath my pillow a few days ago. It's a thoughtful, kind gift that shows just how well Tagiz knows me.

And my heart breaks a little more every time I look at it. If I were smart, I'd give it back.

But I'm not.

Jozet clamps his mouth shut at whatever he sees on my face, following me back to the healers' kradi where he checks on Hewex and then leaves us both with a murmured goodbye.

I get to work, and I'm lost in grinding, cutting, and mixing when Tagiz storms in, his expression fierce.

My heart leaps into my throat as I greedily drink him in. A small part of me is relieved to see he seems to be sleeping about as well as I am, dark circles beneath his eyes.

Eyes that turn sharp as they narrow on me.

He storms forward, ignoring the way everyone in the kradi goes silent as he grabs my elbow, pulling me further toward the back of the kradi.

"Don't leave," he says. "Please, Zoey."

I look at him wide-eyed. "What are you talking about?"

"Hewex told me you're going to leave as soon as the ship is fixed. Just give me one chance, little healer."

I've said no such thing, and I barely control my eyes,

which want to dart in Hewex's direction. The grouchy warrior has obviously decided to give his friend a little encouragement.

A small part of me is enjoying the look of desperation on Tagiz's face. After so long of *me* being the one pining for *him*, I have to admit it's not the worst thing to experience the opposite. But I quite simply don't think I can trust him with my heart.

"Tagiz—"

"I know I don't deserve it. But I can make you happy, little healer. I can give you the kind of love you deserve. You'll never find that kind of love with another male. I swear it."

My heart flips in my chest, and I open my mouth to at least tell him I have no plans to leave...right now.

He clamps his hand over my mouth, and I growl at him.

"Don't decide now." His eyes are frantic. "Give me some time to prove to you how much I need you. And how happy I can make you."

He's gone before I can reply, and I'm left staring after him in bemusement. Hewex rolls onto his side, and I raise my eyebrow at him.

"What exactly did you say to him?"

"The boy needed to realize you weren't going to stay here and wait for him forever."

I sigh. "Since when do you care about our love lives?"

"Since I'm sick of hearing the camp gossip. 'Will they,' 'won't they,' 'should they'—it's tiresome."

"Tiresome. Uh-huh. And how much did you bet on us getting together?"

He scowls at me in offense.

I raise one eyebrow, waiting.

"Ten credits," he mutters. "But only because I know

you'll be mated soon. It's easy to see you're meant to be together."

I swallow around the sudden lump in my throat. "Aw, Hewex. I never realized you were such a romantic."

He gives me a look that suggests I'm a grade A idiot and closes his eyes.

I spend the rest of the day mixing the wrong ingredients together, continually ruining my salves and tonics and starting again.

I'm so distracted I can barely work, and this tiny, burgeoning *hope* is almost worse than the low-level depression that has plagued me for days.

I snort. "You're pathetic," I mutter, furiously grinding a paste until it's closer to water than the smooth salve it should be.

"What was that, child?"

I jump, realizing Moni is working nearby. I didn't even notice I wasn't at the workstation alone.

"Nothing."

Moni gives me a look. "You know, sometimes, the fear of history repeating itself can make you afraid to take risks. You can lose more than you ever thought possible if you are afraid to risk your heart."

I blink back tears. "I don't want to talk about it."

She tilts her head, waiting, and I finally sigh, pushing away the salve.

"My love for Tagiz hurts, Moni. I always thought love would feel good. But this love is brutal and mean. It's wrapped in jealousy, and it makes me feel small."

"Is it your love that makes you feel small? Or is it the thoughts you have about that love?"

I frown at that. Moni has a way of twisting things and making them sound like wisdom. I'm onto her tricks.

She smiles at me as if she's reading my mind. "Will you deprive yourself of love because it wasn't handed to you the way you wanted it? Because when you found it, it wasn't perfect? Will you spend your life wishing you had tried a little more, fought a little harder?"

Tears spill over now, and Moni takes my arm, leading me to a quiet spot near the back of the kradi.

She tuts, wiping away one of my tears. "Go rest, Zoey. You look tired."

I sigh. When Moni says you're dismissed, you're dismissed. I nod, collecting my first aid kit, which I restocked with the things I need, and wander out of the kradi. I don't rest though. I'm a glutton for punishment because I head toward the training arena, desperate for a glimpse of the warrior who makes my heart beat like a drum even as he steals my breath.

I watch him train, careful to stay out of sight. At one point, he seems to feel me watching him because his head swings wildly, his eyes searching the crowd gathered around the training arena. But I duck my head until Terex grabs his attention again and hustle back to my kradi, where I curl up in my furs with Harry.

***

Tagiz

My hand burns as I collect the bright flowers into a large bunch. I frown but shrug, reaching for a few more. Everything hurts when it comes to my little healer. Why should the flowers I pick for her be any different?

It was Beth who suggested the flowers. She said on Earth, males give their females flowers for special occasions.

She tilted her head and also advised me they were a good option for when males were "in the dog house."

Whatever that means.

I can see why Zoey likes to be out here, alone in the forest. I want to end the threat that the Dokhalls present so she can once more have the freedom to gather her plants and herbs alone.

Although, if I can convince her to be mine, perhaps she would allow me to come with her sometimes.

Zoey is in the healers' kradi when I arrive. I smile at her, presenting the flowers, but my smile drops as Moni gasps.

Zoey is also not smiling. "Oh, Tagiz. What did you do?"

This is not the reaction I was expecting.

"These flowers are for you. They don't come close to matching your beauty, but the color reminds me of your eyes."

She chews on her lip, and strangely, she doesn't look pleased. She looks...concerned. Did I misunderstand Beth? Is this ritual not correct?

"Okay, Romeo," she finally sighs, taking a large bowl. "I'm going to need you to drop those flowers in here."

I comply, my brow furrowing. That's when I realize my hand is still on fire.

Zoey sighs. "Moni, can you—"

"Yes, child."

Moni bustles over as Zoey gestures for me to hold out my hand. They pour water over it, and Zoey's hands are gentle as she examines it.

The burning is worsening, angry red blisters rising on my skin.

"This flower is poisonous," Zoey murmurs, gazing up at me through thick lashes. My heart stutters as I glance down at her beautiful face. I have chosen the wrong flower, but the pain is worth it to be this close to her once more. I want to take her mouth with mine, pull her to me and—

"Ahem." Moni shuffles forward again, handing Zoey a salve she has been mixing. I wrinkle my nose at the stench, and Zoey laughs, the sound musical.

"Yes," she says. "It stinks. But it's the only thing that will relieve the pain."

She slathers the greasy salve on my palm carefully. "This needs to be bandaged, I'm afraid. Didn't you notice it was hurting?"

I shrug. "The flowers reminded me of your eyes," I say again.

She sighs. "I'm surprised you didn't know better. You guys are always out in the forest hunting." Her eyes narrow at me, and I tilt my head.

"We know which berries not to eat, which nuts are best left alone, and which fruit is likely to give us a bad stomach. Most warriors pay no attention to plants and flowers."

Her lips twitch. "You're not going to be able to use this hand for a few days."

"It's not my sword hand. I can still protect you."

A tiny flush kisses her cheeks, and I watch, entranced by the color on her soft skin.

"Tagiz...you shouldn't be doing these things. We broke up."

"Broke up?" I frown. "Nothing is broken, little healer."

She sighs again. "Yes, it is."

"Malis and Heric are to be mated tonight."

Her eyes meet mine, her expression startled.

"Tagiz—"

"I told you, little healer. We are no longer at the mercy of our parents. Our destinies are our own."

Zoey

After burning his hand with the xuri flower, Tagiz seems to become even more determined to talk to me. Malis has indeed mated with her warrior, and she's glowing with happiness as she walks around camp.

Tagiz leaves me gifts every day. A pretty rock he knows I'll like. A new collar for Harry. A sharp knife to replace the dull one I left in the forest. Tiny, perfectly carved bowls and boxes to keep my herbs and flowers organized.

People are beginning to talk, taking bets on what he'll leave me next. More than one warrior has suggested I "put him out of his misery," and a few of the new women have suggested that if I don't want him, they'll take him instead.

They stopped suggesting that when I casually mentioned just how proficient I am with poisons.

I wouldn't really poison them, of course. But word got out I'm teetering on the edge of insanity, and most of the women began minding their own business after that.

Not my friends though. No, they're taking their own bets on the situation and giving me unwanted advice from all directions.

Nevada told me to make him crawl. Ellie advised me to beg *his* forgiveness. Beth suggested I talk it out at least, and Ivy said if she has to hear any more about it, she'll do something that would make the evening news on Earth.

Tagiz has also made it clear any male who walks with me into the forest will be meeting him in the training arena.

I allow him to walk with me. Each day, he asks if I will speak to him.

Each day, I tell him no.

It kills me to do this to him. To do this to us. But I lost myself for a while, and now I'm finding myself again.

Since I landed on Agron, I've been a victim, a patient, a healer, a murderer, and now, I guess, a toxicologist.

And this whole time, I've been so in love with Tagiz I could barely see straight. It's not that I enjoy seeing Tagiz beg for my attention; it's that I'm trying to figure out who I am—both with and without him.

But staying away from him is killing me, and Moni's words play over and over again in my head.

"Will you deprive yourself of love because it wasn't handed to you the way you wanted it? Because when you found it, it wasn't perfect? Will you spend your life wishing you had tried a little more, fought a little harder?"

I know better than most people just how short life is. I came so close to death that sometimes I still wake up and almost cry when it no longer hurts to take a full breath.

Mom wouldn't want me to miss out on love because I was afraid. She would never want me to be second best, sure, but at her heart, she was someone who believed fiercely in love.

Wherever she is, I'm sure she's urging me to conquer my fear and grab love with both hands.

So that's what I'm going to do.

CHAPTER NINETEEN

Z oey

Surprisingly, it's Malis I go to for help putting my plan into motion. She throws her arms around me, talking a mile a minute, and we end up chatting for hours, as if we've been friends for years.

"I'm so happy you're doing this, Zoey. I know it's difficult after everything that's happened, but I've never seen anyone love someone the way Tagiz loves you."

I blink back tears at that, and she smiles at me. "It's hard, isn't it? Being brave enough to take the leap. But as someone who finally jumped...it's worth it. And I promise, Tagiz will be there to catch you."

Tagiz isn't in the training arena when I go looking for him. I finally find him in the healers' kradi, where Moni is changing the bandage on his hand, and my heart flips in my chest at the reminder of the flowers he brought me.

"How's it looking?" I ask as I approach, and Tagiz's free

hand whips out, pulling me close. I allow it, and he looks surprised, although the surprise quickly changes to pure male satisfaction as my breasts are suddenly at his eye level.

"No permanent damage," Moni says. "Three more days of the bandage and then it can come off. And maybe this warrior will learn not to pick poisonous flowers, hmm?"

Tagiz grins at me. "It was worth it."

Butterflies are swarming in my stomach, and I blow out a breath. "Can I talk to you?"

His grin drops, and his gaze searches my face. I hate that I've put that uncertainty in his eyes.

He nods, dropping my hand and getting to his feet. From the set of his shoulders, I'm pretty sure he thinks I'm going to ask him to leave me alone.

"Take me to the stream?"

He tenses further, and I sigh. I bet he doesn't want to ruin his favorite place with the memory of me telling him it's over.

"Please?"

He nods, but he won't meet my eyes as he leads me toward the stream. I ignore the whispers and gazes on us as we walk through camp, and then I'm wiping my sweaty hands on my dress as the water rushes past in front of us.

"Tagiz—"

"I know what you're going to say, Zoey, and I understand. You deserve better than the way I treated you. Rakiz has offered me a position as envoy to some of the other tribes who fought with us in the last battle. I won't bother you anymore."

Wait. What?

Panic bubbles in my chest. I'm such an idiot. I waited too long, and now I've lost him.

"Tagiz—"

"It's okay, little healer. I only wish I had not taken so long to see what was in front of my face. You are the most incredible female I have ever known, and I will wait for you...even if you never choose me, I will be waiting."

I blink at that.

"Tagiz—"

"I will leave—"

"Tagiz!"

I cut him off, and he frowns at me. I hoped to do this in a much more romantic way, but the idea of him leaving...

No.

I thrust my hand into my pocket and pull out the gold mating bands. Malis helped me make them, and it seemed oddly fitting she would contribute to the design.

Tagiz stares at me, and I swallow around the lump in my throat.

"Do you still want me?"

He strides toward me, pulling me into his arms. "Tell me you're serious, little healer."

I nod. "I'm sorry it took so long for me to get it. I have shit in my past that made it difficult for me to trust you. But I *do*. Trust you, I mean. I trust you more than anyone I've ever met. You helped me live—in every way that counts. You gave me something to live *for*, and I was so scared, so fucking terrified I was going to lose you, that I shut down. I could barely look at you because the thought of you being mated to someone else, even if you didn't want it..."

Tears are rolling down my face, and Tagiz wipes away each one, his expression fierce.

"I would wait a lifetime for you, little healer. I would wait until I was about to take my last breath if I knew your face would be the last thing I see."

I hiccup out a sob, and he smiles down at me. Then he

wraps those strong arms around me, surrounding me with his citrus-and-wood scent. I nuzzle in close, and something in my chest relaxes.

"God," I manage to get out. And then I just stand there, surrounded by him as he leans down and rests his chin on my head, blocking out the whole universe.

He gives me a few moments before stepping back and swinging me up until I'm cradled in his arms.

I shriek as my feet leave the ground. "What are you doing?"

"Taking you back to my kradi before you change your mind."

I laugh. "I'm not changing my mind, you fool. Put me down."

I gaze up at his face, and his lower lip juts out just the tiniest bit at my demand as he strides away from the stream and toward the kradis.

I want to bite it.

"You're mine now," he says. "That means you live with me."

"Whoa, someone is turning into a caveman."

He stops and stares down at me. "You said you were mine."

I raise one hand, trailing it over the scruff of his cheek. "I am."

"Good." He continues walking.

I manage to block out the curious eyes on us because I'm so damn entranced by the mix of stubborn determination and obvious lust on his face.

Within a couple of minutes, he's stepping into his kradi and striding straight to the furs where we first made love.

My heart is beating so hard I can hear it in my ears. I'm

panting out each breath, and I reach for him as he reaches for me, desperate to feel him inside me.

He takes my mouth, and I revel in the feel of him. His tongue strokes against mine, his hand cupping my head, holding me in place for him. I raise my hands to pull him even closer, and he catches my wrists in one of his hands.

I moan out a protest, and he chuckles against my mouth, slowly moving away. His eyes are as dark as I've ever seen them and full of triumph.

He raises my hands over my head until I'm clutching at a pillow above me.

"Hold on and don't let go."

I pout, wanting to rip his clothes off, and he leans down and nips at my lower lip.

"Do you trust me?"

"You know I do."

"Then keep your hands up there."

It takes all my self-control not to move my hands as he begins stripping off his clothes. And I let out a sound as he turns to my dress, slowly pulling it off my body. I raise my hands, just to see what he'll do, and he instantly presses them back down.

"Next time I'll tie them," he warns.

We both blink at the moan that leaves my throat at that idea.

He throws his head back and laughs. Moments later, he's wrapping some kind of material around my wrists and looping it around something above my head. It's loose enough I can escape if I need to, but the look in Tagiz's eyes...

I've never been wetter.

He lets out a growl as he finishes removing my dress, his

mouth immediately exploring my breasts. One hand finds the soaked heat of me, and he meets my eyes as I blush.

"You're perfect."

He doesn't waste any time, moving his head down until his lips are grazing my clit and my thighs are clenching as I groan. He laps at me, teasing me until I'm begging for more, and then he pushes one large finger inside me, swirling his tongue around my clit like he'll never get enough.

I want to bury my hands in his hair and pull him closer, and I twist my hips, but I'm completely powerless.

It's that thought that makes me explode, his name falling from my lips as the orgasm rips through my body.

I'm still trembling from the aftershocks when he slides inside me, not stopping until he's buried deep and I'm filled with him. He presses kisses against my face and then moves, driving his hips and grinding into my clit with each thrust.

I lose track of time, only focused on the feeling of him deep within me, driving me higher and higher. His gaze meets mine, and my throat tightens. I'm going to be staring into those eyes every day for the rest of my life.

He takes my mouth again, twisting his hips, and I gasp out a curse.

"Oh God, oh God, oh God," I chant, already close to coming again. He laughs, but the sound is strangled, and I throw my head back, clamping down around him. I shake through the best orgasm of my life as he empties himself inside me, burying his head in my shoulder as I attempt to catch my breath.

Z oey

I glance up from my worktable as someone calls my name.

"Ellie! How are you?"

She grins at me. "Deep in thought?"

I laugh as I continue mixing the salve I'm working on. "I have a meeting with Nevada and Rakiz later. Just thinking about what to do about the Dokhalls. There was another attack today. Weirdly, they're not going near the ship right now. Maybe it's too well guarded and they're hoping if they annoy Rakiz and Dexar enough, they'll hand it over."

Ellie snorts. "If that's what they think, they haven't been paying attention to the Braxians. Oh wow, you're getting so big."

I glance up from the bowl I'm stirring with a frown. Thankfully, it's not me she's talking to. It's Harry, who is currently curled up under my worktable. He followed me to the healers' kradi a few days ago and has now obviously decided this is his place. Moni shook her head disapprovingly but muttered that as long as he stayed away from the patients, he could "guard his human."

Apparently, karja are some of the cleanest animals on Agron.

"Yeah, it's kind of insane how fast he's growing. You can pet him if you want."

Ellie nibbles her lip as she stares at the karja, who opens one eye, a tiny growl escaping his throat as if he's ordering her to get on with it. Finally, she strokes along his fuzzy head, laughing as he butts it against her hand, looking for more.

"You guys are leaving soon, right?" Ellie looks sad, and I nudge her.

"It's not for long. We'll be back and forth."

I insisted Tagiz take the envoy position under one condition—I could go with him. So in a few days, we'll go rendezvous with Khax and his warriors and see who else will continue to ally with us against the Dokhalls. The best part? We're finally going to the Seinex Forest so I can collect some of the herbs, plants, flowers, and mushrooms that grow there.

"I'm still going to miss you. But for now, I need you to come with me," Ellie says.

I raise one eyebrow, but she's already gesturing to Moni, who nods. My heart flips in my chest. "Has something happened? Is it Tagiz?"

"No, no, nothing like that. Just come with me and don't ask any questions."

"Jeez. This is some cloak-and-dagger stuff right here. Okay, then."

Harry gets to his feet and follows us as we leave the healers' kradi. It's already getting dark outside, the days getting shorter. Soon, we'll have our first winter on Agron.

I'm so lost in thought it takes me a moment to realize where Ellie is taking me.

"You know about this spot too?"

She nods. "I sneak over here when no one is looking." We pass through the last clump of trees before the stream, and my breath shudders from my lungs.

Candles. And flowers. Everywhere.

Nevada and Beth grin at me as I pass them, and other than Vivian, all my human friends are squeezed into this tiny space. Rakiz nods at me, his daughter in his arms, and my heart pounds even harder as I meet Tagiz's mom's eyes.

She beams at me, and I blink at her, confused. She leans forward as I approach her, wrapping her arms around me.

"Tagiz has told me so much about you," she murmurs. "I can't wait to have you as a daughter, Zoey."

All I can do is gape at her, and her smile widens as she steps back. She nods toward the stream, and I turn to where Tagiz is waiting for me.

He looks nervous.

I still have our mating bands in our kradi. We're waiting until Vivian is back and the Dokhall threat is ended. So what's going on?

I practically sprint toward Tagiz, and the crowd erupts into laughter as he lifts me into his arms and spins me around. Harry nudges at Tagiz, demanding attention until he pats him on the head, and then the karja loses interest, wandering away.

"What's going on?" I ask, and Tagiz gives me the crooked grin I love so much.

And then he drops down onto one knee.

Holy shit.

He reaches for my left hand, and I'm so stunned all I can do is stare at him as he holds up a gleaming gold ring.

"Zoey, I love you more than I ever thought possible. I can't wait to mate with you in the way of my people. But I want more than that. I want everything. I want to be your *husband*." He stumbles over the English word slightly, and tears prick my eyes. "I want you to be my *wife*." He does better there, and tears begin rolling down my face. "I want to be tied to you in all ways, including the ways of your people. Will you marry me?"

I'm sobbing now, but I let out a strangled sound that he obviously takes as a yes because he pushes the gleaming gold band onto my ring finger.

He gets to his feet, taking my lips as cheers sound around us.

"Where...how...what?"

His eyes laugh at me. "I talked to your human friends. I convinced Dragix to take me to Arix's marketplace so I could purchase the ring."

I blink at him. "That was before we were even back together."

He nods. "I knew I wanted everything from you, Zoey. I would have waited as long as it took."

"How did I get so lucky?" I murmur, and he laughs.

Harry returns, nudging us with his head until we give him the attention he feels he deserves. Moments later, we're surrounded by our friends, our *family*, as they congratulate us.

I don't know what life holds for us on Agron. We have another war brewing and enemies around every corner. But whatever comes, I'll face it with Tagiz by my side.

And he's worth everything.

. . .

The End

Authors Note:

Thanks for reading Rescued by the Alien Warrior. At its core, this story is about leaving behind the person you thought you were, and embracing the person you truly are.

It's never easy, but it's always worth it. And sometimes, while leaving the past behind, you embrace the future with the person you were always supposed to be with.

If you enjoyed Rescued, I'd love if you could take a moment to leave a review. These help other readers find my books.

Want to be the first to know about new releases, along with audiobooks, freebies, and more? Sign up for my free newsletter here.

I'm also active on Facebook. Come say hi at Hope Hart Author.

Vivian and Arix's story is up next and you won't want to miss it! Keep reading for a sneak peek of Enticed by the Alien Warrior.

ENTICED BY THE ALIEN
WARRIOR

Vivian

W*e're defined by our actions. By the things we do when no one is watching. By the way we behave when we're only accountable to ourselves.*

But most importantly, we're defined by the steps we take when saving ourselves means harm to someone else.

What do you do when your back is against the wall?

Either way, I will be forever defined by the choice I'm about to make. And there's one thing that no one tells you about those difficult, life-defining actions. Others may judge you, but they get to walk away. You're the one who has to live with yourself.

Arix

I watch the small human females as they walk toward my castle. Vivian smiles, and I can't help but stare. From the moment my eyes met hers so many days ago, I was entranced. Her beauty makes her seem cool, almost icy, but I have no doubt that beneath the composure she wears like a mask is a female who burns with the hottest blue flame.

"I don't like this," Korzyn murmurs. "I don't trust them."

I glance over my shoulder at where my commander is leaning against the wall, his eyes also on the two human females.

"You don't trust anyone."

He shrugs. "That may be true, but I especially don't trust females who may have been planted here by your enemies. You have no true alliance with the barbarians across the water. What if they have been sent here to gather intelligence and report back?"

I wave a hand, turning back to where Vivian is throwing her head back with laughter at something the other female says. I have a sudden urge to lean out the window so I can hear the sound.

"What intelligence can they gather? I've assigned guards to them, and they won't be walking around the castle unattended."

"What if they're here to kill you?"

As the females move into the castle and out of my view, I sigh, turning back to the male who has been staunchly at my side since the day my parents died and I picked up my father's crown.

"You believe those tiny females could kill me?"

His frown deepens. "They could be used as a distraction."

There have been numerous attempts on my life over the years. While my parents' deaths are officially considered to be accidents, I know the truth.

They were cold-blooded murders. And I was supposed to be the third victim, leaving my throne up for grabs.

As much as I tease Korzyn for his paranoia, there's no question that that paranoia has kept me alive more times than I can count. And if he has a bad feeling…

"I'll be careful," I say. "I swear it."

All these years, and I still haven't discovered who killed my parents. I have discovered traitors, of course. One of my first orders as king was the execution of the guard who was supposed to be by my parents' side that night but was found attempting to escape my kingdom.

But I've never found the person responsible for making me king before my time. The thought of my revenge is the first thing that crosses my mind when I open my eyes in the morning and the last thing when I close them at night.

My gaze clings to Vivian's face as I push the thought of my parents away. I want the little human. I've wanted her since the moment I laid my eyes on her. She's beautiful and brave, and something about the way she holds herself makes me think she might be broken.

Like me.

But that's all this is. I want to lose myself in her body, cut myself on her sharp edges. I want to roll her across my sheets and spread her hair along my pillow. And then, when I am finished with her, I will kiss her goodbye and send her on her way when she leaves my planet. Forever.

Vivian

My stomach is tense as Sarissa and I hug Zoey goodbye.

"Are you sure about this?" she asks again as Hewex and Tagiz frown disapprovingly.

I throw them a wink. "Positive."

She looks doubtful, but if I'm going in, I'm going all in.

Sarissa raises her eyebrow at me, but she picks up what I'm throwing at her, giving Zoey a wide smile.

"This is an excellent idea. We'll be in touch as soon as we've gotten this part fixed."

Tagiz practically has to drag Zoey away, but she finally gives us one last hug, and my cousin and I are suddenly alone on the "other" side of the Colossal Water.

I slide Sarissa a look. "This was a smart decision, right?" I ask.

My cousin shrugs. "Girl, I was just going along with whatever plan you'd cooked up."

I narrow my eyes at her, and she grins, nudging me with her shoulder. "I'm not saying it's a bad plan, just that I practically got whiplash from your decision-making process."

I sigh. Okay, so I may have a rather large chip on my shoulder about contributing to the cause. I've spent most of my time on Agron being a distraction while the other women got shit done. Now it's my turn to help us get our ship fixed so we can finally get off this planet.

Not that this planet is bad. It's barbaric, that's for sure, although the Braxians have treated us like family since the moment Rakiz's tribe rescued us. But when you're plucked from your life without any warning, you'll do just about anything to get that life back.

"Well," I say as we turn and follow the guards toward the giant obsidian castle, "decision made. No turning back now."

We have a lead on someone who can fix the thruster from our ship, but apparently the guy only visits Agron sporadically. Hence why we're here.

Arix—the king on this side of the Colossal Water—has

already left to do whatever it is he does. For now, his guards are going to show us to our rooms.

Rooms. In a castle.

Yeah, whiplash is right. Before this, we were sleeping in kradis—comfortable, clean tents, but tents just the same. This is a life upgrade, although I already miss the other women. Nevada and Ellie are both pregnant and due to pop any day, and I've become close with Zoey and even a few of the new human women who were trapped in a cage on the ship full of Dokhalls that attempted to take us back.

We leave the dock behind and enter the castle from the back, clomping up the black stone steps and along silver tiles that are so polished I can see my reflection in them. Our footsteps echo as we file down the hallway until we're back in the main entrance hall. I can't help but gaze up.

There are some places that make you feel small. The Grand Canyon. The redwood parks in California. The open ocean.

This castle is like that.

It's made of some kind of black stone, but the word *black* doesn't do it justice. It's so dark that it seems to absorb the light, reflecting it back in the gleaming veins of silver that peek out here and there.

It would be gloomy and depressing if not for the massive windows above us, providing the natural light throughout the hall.

One of the guards clears his throat, and I glance at Sarissa. Both of us are standing here with our mouths open as we examine the entrance hall. I laugh.

"We're like a couple of small-town girls in the big city for the first time," I mutter, and she grins.

We follow the guards up the massive staircase, which leads to a landing. Above us, more corridors intersect, cutting through the air above and below one another in a dizzying pattern. People are hurrying down those corridors, a few of them glancing at us curiously, but they've obviously got places to go because no one pauses.

By the time the guards stop outside a silver door, I'm completely and utterly lost, and I can tell by the tiny line between Sarissa's eyebrows that she feels the same.

"Do you guys have some kind of map we can use while we're here?" she asks.

The guard smiles, but it doesn't reach his eyes. "We will escort you anywhere you need to go."

Sarissa and I share a glance. Arix referred to us as his guests. But if he expects guards to be with us each time we leave our rooms, it seems we're really more like prisoners.

She nods, a silent agreement that we'll discuss this later. The guard opens the door and gestures her in, and he stays behind to show her through the room, while another guard opens the next door down for me.

At least we'll be close to each other.

"This is your sitting room, and through that door, you'll find your bathing room." He strides to the right, opening another door. "Bedroom. Please pull the cord by the door if you need anything and a servant will come to help you."

The suite is gorgeous. I wander into the bedroom, my mouth gaping at the size of the bed. A vanity sits by an open closet, and I frown.

"Is this someone else's room?"

The guard tilts his head. "I'm not sure what you mean."

"The clothes..."

"They're for you."

I feel a little like Alice, and I've just fallen down the rabbit hole. I stride to the closet and pull out one of the dresses. It looks like it'll fit perfectly. But Arix had no way of knowing we'd stay here. Did he?

"Thank you," I murmur, and the guard nods, backing out of the room.

Moments later, Sarissa appears, nodding at the dress I'm still holding. "It's weird, huh?"

"Braxian women are so much taller than us. It's like he had these dresses made in advance."

"I've said it before, and I'll say it again. I don't trust him."

Sarissa works for the CIA. And no, I have no idea what she does. She clams up every time I ask about it, so I'm pretty sure she's not allowed to talk about what her day-to-day tasks actually are.

I blow out a breath. "Look, no matter his reasons for wanting us here, we know why *we* want to be here. If we can get the thruster fixed and find someone to replace that chip...we could be out of here within a few weeks. Let's keep our eye on the prize."

Sarissa nods, wandering over to my bed and running her hand over the ruby-red velvet blanket draped over the end. "I'll get to work on an escape plan," she murmurs, "just in case."

Click here to read Enticed by the Alien Warrior.

ALSO BY HOPE HART

The Arcav Alien Invasion Series

The Arcav King's Mate

The Arcav Commander's Human

The Arcav General's Woman

The Arcav Prince's Captive

A Very Arcav Christmas

The Arcav Captain's Queen

The Arcav Guard's Female

The Warriors of Agron Series

Taken by the Alien Warrior

Claimed by the Alien Warrior

Saved by the Alien Warrior

Seduced by the Alien Warrior

Protected by the Alien Warrior

Captured by the Alien Warrior

Rescued by the Alien Warrior

Enticed by the Alien Warrior

Conquered by the Alien Warrior